D0965749

THE NIGHT
OF THE GIRAFFE
& Other Stories

Alfred Andersch

THE NIGHT
OF THE GIRAFFE

& Other Stories

Translated from the German by
CHRISTA ARMSTRONG

Pantheon Books
A Division of Random House
New York

Fic
AND

Contents

THE NIGHT
OF THE GIRAFFE
& Other Stories

The Night of the Giraffe

ON THE NIGHT of May 29 at eleven o'clock—that is, at the same time as I was having dinner in a small restaurant on the Rue des Saints-Pères—an Algerian of about twenty-five whose name I never learned sat down at a table outside a café on the Rue Monge to wait for my friend Pierre Grange. The young Algerian had carefully picked this café. From where he sat he could command the intersection of the Rue Monge, the Rue Cardinal-Lemoine, and the Rue des Boulangers where Pierre lived, and also the exit of the Metro station Cardinal-Lemoine. He carried three new ten-thousand-franc notes which he had received from the agent of a French fascist organization. They were

tucked in a thin, worn leather wallet inside the breast
pocket of his black tunic. A few coins and a pack of cigarettes were in the right pocket of his trousers. An oblong
pocket which he himself had sewn inside the right leg of
his corduroy trousers held a knife with a ten-inch blade,
grooved on four sides—a stiletto, in other words, which
ended in a point almost as sharp as a needle. He was
unbelievably thin according to our standards, like all
young North Africans; slim, sinewy, small and dark he sat
in front of the café. He had ordered a Pinard and had paid
for it at once. The white cigarette gleamed in his brown
hands. Slumped into himself, completely calm and slightly
dirty, he sat there and waited. Before he came he had tele-
phoned the agent from one of the big Negro cafés on the
Boul Mich and found out that my friend Pierre was sitting
in the Deux Magots. The agent had thought Pierre
Grange might be late in getting home. So the Algerian
waited placidly. Of course, I knew nothing of his existence
as I sat in the bistro on the Rue des Saints-Pères eating a
cutlet, pommes frites and a salad and reading the latest
edition of the *Herald Tribune*. But in view of all that
happened later that night I can easily picture the vigil of
this dirty little hired guy. Just as I had finished my dinner,
shortly after eleven, the cars began honking outside. We—
that is, the four or five guests in the bistro and the patron—
pricked up our ears, for blowing horns is strictly forbidden
in Paris at night. The cars were all honking the same
signal, three short and one long blast. The patron went
to the door, looked out into the street and said: "A demonstration." I paid my check, clutched the papers under my
arm and left. Outside the air was heavy.

On the evening of the same day, May 29, at 7:26 to be
exact, the tall old General's tall old Citroën passed into the

courtyard of the Élysée Palace through the gate opened only on visits of foreign heads of state. Exactly twenty-four hours before, 350,000 people between the Place de la République and the Bastille had protested against this visit. One of the Presidential footmen opened the door of the car, but the General did not get out at once. Instead he leaned forward a little and asked his driver: "René, what are the latest slogans?" " 'Into the museum with de Gaulle,' " the driver replied. This is what they hate about me most, the General thought, the fact that I don't fit in with their time. They cannot understand that time adjusts to him who makes it. But I shall be king in France. Come to think of it, nothing has changed at all since the days of the kings. Kings of France are always caught between the Huguenots and the League, between the liberal opposition and the military gang. The Huguenots expect a St. Bartholomew's Night from me. But I am not a juvenile king who has a gray-haired Protestant admiral assassinated. I am gray-haired myself and I respect that little Jew who led the masses across the Bastille yesterday. It was he who saved the honor of France in Indochina. He is probably just as alone among his people as I am among mine. Yet, I must fight him. The Pope cannot be a Ghibelline. But I shall have the estates of the heads of the League confiscated, he thought grimly. "And what else?" he asked. The driver, he noticed, hesitated for a second. "Come on, René, I want to know what they say about me." " 'Into the zoo with the giraffe,' " the chauffeur said. He looked into the mirror but could detect no emotion on the General's face. A stupid word, thought the General, it cannot possibly come from the clever little Jew. The little Jew would know what would happen if they started locking giraffes into the zoo. If they locked up tall old generals they would also lock up clever little Jews and soon anybody who did not fit in with

*the time would be locked up. Into this time, the General
thought with contempt, and finally stepped out of the car.
He really has something of the giraffe, thought the driver
admiringly, watching his general reach the top of the stairs
and lean down to the President of the Republic, who had
already been waiting up there for some time.*

pages from the original manuscript of proust's "à la
recherche du temps perdu" in the windows of the librairie
la hune. also galley proofs with the author's corrections;
he has written whole new paragraphs onto the margins.
across the street at the montana bar the american smart set
from the 6th arrondissement: elegant fairies mainly.
juliette-greco shadows on the lower lids of dazzling girls.
the serious journalist crowd at le village. café-au-lait colored half-caste girl in brown leather jacket, only her thighs
shining in white pants glued to the skin, escorted by three
men. kenny clarke at the traps in the st-germain-des-prés
club playing with a french master pianist before five guests,
the bottle of coke at a thousand francs. sartre's apartment
on the corner of the rue bonaparte is all lit up. the deux
magots newsstand sparkling like a jewel in the blue night
of bobbing street lights. marianne puts her head on the
block and lets the guillotine down on herself: the cartoon
from "punch" heading the latest edition of "l'express."
tomato-red alfa-romeo convertible wedged in on the rue
st-bénoit. green drinks, white drinks, green drinks on the
tables seen through yellow coffee-house windows in the
dove-blue night. but houses and church, velvety brown and
feathery gray, flickered over by street lights. the surface of
paris equals the Depth of Paris. troubled arthur adamov
walking along the boulevard in conversation with martin
flinker. "que voulez-vous," the seventy-year-old bookseller,
one of the century's hounded creatures, says to adamov,
"one can never live through too many historical events."

"You do remember, don't you, Fayard, that I was in Algeria with Chaban-Delmas?"

"I do, now you mention it, Grange. That was at the time when Chaban-Delmas was Defense Minister under Gaillard."

"Quite right. And that was only three months ago."

"So you were in Algeria in the spring."

"In February."

"Was it a nice trip?"

"Listen, Fayard, I didn't ask to see you to tell you whether or not February is a nice month in Algeria."

"But . . .?"

"Did you ever hear the name Léon Delbecque?"

"You're kidding!"

"I only asked because Delbecque's name isn't often mentioned in the Paris press. Even in your paper, Fayard."

"Everybody knows Delbecque prepared the plot in Algiers, but nobody can prove it."

"I can."

"Not really!"

"You don't seem to be exactly panting for information, or am I wrong?"

"You have the wrong idea about journalism, Grange, but go ahead. I know you are sound. You got on Chaban-Delmas's staff via the Navy Department, didn't you?"

"Yes, it's funny. I am only a civilian employee in the Department, you know, just a bread-and-butter job which leaves me time to work on my magazine and the theater reviews for your paper. But then somebody had the idea to assign me to a rear admiral and have me carry his brief-case to Algeria."

"You think that was just a coincidence?"

"Of course."

"I believe you underestimate the Navy Department. But go on."

"I happened to meet Delbecque on the trip. As you know, he was personal assistant to the Minister. It was so interesting to watch him, I ended up doing nothing else."

"And what did you see?"

"Wherever we stopped, Delbecque held secret conferences with the local military and civilian officials. The Minister made a public speech while his assistant gave private instructions."

"Well, that's common knowledge. We all know it."

"But no one can prove it."

"The people of the Welfare Commission at Algiers will tell anybody who cares to ask and Delbecque won't dream of denying the gossip."

"But it remains a rumor?"

"Yes, it's the typical scuttlebutt—an item for today's gossip and tomorrow's historians."

"It needn't remain that."

"Don't make it too exciting, Grange. I've known for the last five minutes that you wish to present me with proof of Delbecque's activities, all signed and sealed."

"Right. I have made an accurate list of nearly all of Delbecque's meetings, including the names of everyone participating."

"Do you also know what was discussed on those occasions?"

"No. I leave the rest to the journalists. There is a group of about a hundred and fifty persons involved."

"And what do you want me to do?"

"Publish the list!"

"What good would that do?"

"But don't you understand, the list is plain proof that the plot has been prepared long beforehand."

"Whose hand?"

"You ask strange questions. All insiders know Delbecque is Jacques Soustelle's agent. And everyone in France knows Soustelle is de Gaulle's political whip. My list will prove that the General himself has had the plot prepared against the Republic. The great taciturn of Colombey, the impeccable man of honor who waits until he is called. At best a political manipulator like any other. At worst a political criminal working against the legitimacy of the Republic."

"I'm not going to publish your list, Grange."

"And why not?"

"Because our editorial board has just decided to give the giraffe a chance."

"You mean you have decided in favor of opportunism?"

"Well, let's assume for the moment the publication of your list would have the effect you visualize. What would be the result?"

"That's easy to see, isn't it? De Gaulle's myth would be destroyed or, let's say, slightly damaged."

"Right! And that's exactly what we don't want. At least not now."

"That's interesting! I've never heard you take the part of a myth yet, Fayard. You are a left-wing citizen. You publish a left-wing bourgeois paper. So far, you've always been on the side of reason."

"Myth plays an objective part in politics."

"But if it can be unmasked . . ."

"It will have to unmask itself. De Gaulle himself must destroy his legend."

"And if he doesn't oblige?"

"Then his myth is genuine."

"You mean in that case de Gaulle is a man of honor after all?"

"We must give him the chance to prove it."

"Even though my list proves he has already violated the rules of honor?"

"There's a chance he may be playing for high stakes, a game for our side, a game against the Delbecques."

"But that's an illusion."

"And if it isn't?"

"Then everything you and your paper have stood for would have been wrong—your talk about democracy and the rule of the people, the meaning of universal suffrage and the lucidity of politics. Then politics would be what your conservative opponents teach: the private affair of individuals, depending on the honor or dishonor of never-changing human character, a passion or an intrigue, a deal between cliques, a secret web, the maneuvers of gangs or elites who have already made their decisions before the citizen—your citizen, Fayard!—has had even the shadow of a chance to use his influence. True, it is left to him to finance or not finance the water supply of Bordeaux, but the decisions of General de Gaulle are made without him."

"You have completely wrong ideas about the role of public consent or dissent, Grange."

"I am just learning. Obviously, the public's vote is always doomed to be too late."

"Sometimes it may prepare the way. The fact that de Gaulle can come to power is the result of a public vote."

"Before which you capitulate. Which perhaps your own paper manipulated."

"So what! We respect the vote. We never resist developments which can't be stopped. We maintain our principles as things develop, our ideas of freedom and human dignity . . ."

"That's bunk, Fayard."

"You aren't thirty yet, I am fifty. You may go ahead and insult me all you like."

"I shall. From now on I shall insult you and your kind incessantly."

"It won't help you. By the way, why don't you take your list to your friend Sartre, or to *Humanité*?"

"You know very well it wouldn't have ten percent of the effect there that it would have coming from you. It should be published by a paper as dignified and objective as your respectable bourgeois organ, Fayard."

"You're right, of course. You're intelligent, Grange, you're the sort that could adjust to the mechanism of power. I'd like to give you some better advice."

"Well?"

"Burn the list! Don't just burn it—forget it."

"So you're that afraid of de Gaulle?"

"I am not afraid of de Gaulle. Perhaps I am afraid of the Delbecques. But, at the moment, I am only worried about you."

"Thanks a lot!"

"That's a very dangerous paper you have in your pocket, Grange. Some day, perhaps, it will be a very valuable paper. But it will never be so valuable that somebody should die for it."

"I've no answer to that."

"I know. Take care of yourself!"

"Adieu, Fayard."

As I walked down the Boulevard St-Germain, more and more honking cars came by from the direction of the Concorde. All were honking the same signal, the first four notes of Beethoven's Fifth which, as I read in the *Herald Tribune* next morning, had been the victory signal of Winston Churchill and Charles de Gaulle during the war. I also read that the frenzy of Gaullist victory had broken loose that night in the Champs-Élysées: a piercing cry of enthusiasm uttered by ladies with white gloves, the wild roar of young businessmen, the revolution of the car owners, as Pendennis dryly remarked in *The Observer*. The political geography of Paris is simple: the victories of the car owners are celebrated in the Champs-Élysées, contradicted in St-Germain-des-Prés, passed over in silence at Ménilmontant. The three short and one long note were supposed to mean: "Al-gérie Fran-çaise." It was a plain provocation of the intellectuals. Alleg had written the book about his tortures by the paratroopers. Sartre had written a commentary to it. Alleg's book and Sartre's commentary had been banned. Audin, the young mathematician, had died under the tortures of the paras—and St-Germain-des-Prés stood along the two sidewalks of its Boulevard, whistling and yelling above the noise of the horns, dark shapes moving against bright windows and the twitching reflection of lights from its cafés. It was going on half past eleven. Through the turmoil I made for the Deux Magots newsstand to see if the Gaullist poster was still there on the rear wall. But it had been torn off and lay in the gutter soiled and trampled. By this time it had become rather quiet at the corner of the Rue Monge and the Rue Cardinal-Lemoine where the young Algerian sat and waited for my friend Pierre. I saw Pierre sitting in front of the Deux Magots, Solange by his side, and I went to join them. At the table next to Pierre's three Americans had climbed on their chairs for a better view of the rumpus on the street, a lady of forty, shapely and smelling of money, with two rather unprepossessing daughters. A couple of young Frenchmen kidding around with them quipped, "Mesdames—the revolution," while the waiters were already collecting the checks. The patron and the waiters of the Deux Magots were experienced people and I am experienced too, I've had a few little experiences in the way of street fights back in Germany and I figured the police would turn up in half an hour at the latest. They would begin clearing the Boulevard right from the line of the Deux Magots over to the Royal and the cafés would have to have their shutters down by then or they might get slightly wrecked. I communicated my observations to Pierre but noticed only then that he was very quiet, sitting there pensively. I asked him what the matter was and finally Solange told me about Pierre's talk with Fayard. "Listen," I said to Pierre, "Fayard is right in what he says about the danger you are in. What are you going to do about it?" "Fayard is Evil," Pierre said without answering my question. "It's not de Gaulle who is Evil, not even the paras who tortured Alleg. It's Fayard. Fayard or the tactics, the tactical tolerance, the technique of compromise." He grabbed me by the arm all of a sudden and cried: "Democracy is Evil." I said: "You're nuts. First of all Fayard is not Democracy and secondly he may even be right on this thing. Democracy is a technique of compromise, not of the phoney kind of compromise, naturally, but of creative compromise." But Pierre interrupted me and said: "You are phrase mongers, all of you, I want to publish my list." At this moment things really began to happen on the Boulevard. The crowds surged from the sidewalks into the street and closed in on the honking cars. "Come along," I said to Pierre and Solange, "we'll go up to the corner of the Rue Dragon. From there we can make off sideways when the police arrive." But Pierre shook his head and remained where he sat and Solange with him, of course. If there is anything I am scared of it's the police. I acquired that habit in Germany, and with all the things you hear about the police of Paris . . . Meanwhile the young Algerian who waited for Pierre had ordered and paid for his second Pinard. Behind him, inside the café, the patron and a few customers were listening to the latest radio news. If ever there was a man able just to sit without thinking of anything at all it was the young Algerian that night. He waited and thought nothing at all. Now and then he fingered his knife. Nothingness and the knife surrounded by sputtering radio news were waiting for Pierre.

After the President of the Republic had asked the General to form the new government of France, the General left the Élysée Palace at 9:14 p.m. and went to see André Malraux, his closest adviser and confidant. Malraux, intellectual head of the Left in France until about 1937, participant in the Canton revolt and the Spanish War, during that time author of twentieth-century romans à clef, then retiring into the background of politics and literature and devoting himself to the history of art, joined the General in his Paris headquarters at 5 Rue Solferino and drove with him to a friend's country house on the Marne. No reporter was able to follow the General's car and police escort. The night of May 29th was dark. Malraux, sharp and elegant as usual, listened to de Gaulle. They sat facing each other by the fireside. They were alone. "You were absolutely right to demand the votes of the Socialists," Malraux said. The General: "I told Mollet, 'All right, I shall join the government but you are going with me.'" They both smiled contemptuously as Mollet's name was mentioned. "Of course, you know the thing would be to take not Mollet but Mendès-France into the government," Malraux said. De Gaulle nodded. "I have asked Pierre Closterman to sound out Mendès-France," Malraux went on, "you know what close friends they are; Mendès-France was a first lieutenant in Closterman's squadron during the war." The General was delighted to hear the name of the great fighter pilot. "And what is the answer?" "Still nega-

tive so far," Malraux replied. It will remain negative too, thought Charles de Gaulle, Mendès-France would accept anything, even my policy, but what he cannot accept is the Cross of Lorraine. Mendès-France is a Jewish Liberal and I am a Catholic Conservative. We are fire and water. But Malraux, who had been through Marxism and the sacraments, thought: If there is anything that can save us from the terror squads of the Communists and the tortures of the paratroopers, from the impotence of parliaments and the corruption of the press, it will be the alliance of the great Conservatives and the great Liberals, the silent accord of Right and Left, a union of elites against the law of inertia in mass society. I shall restore the old way of making policy in secret, thought de Gaulle, the policy which lets a man keep his character, and that is why Mendès-France must fight me. For Mendès-France wants freedom, not secrecy. He knows that deep inside of what is secret there is the Law, the never-changing Law of the Everlasting, the Cross of Lorraine, just as I know that in the innermost heart of the idea of freedom there is anarchy, the moment when the Law is destroyed, Prometheus bringing the fire down from heaven. In an hour like this the impossible must happen, thought Malraux, the unreconcilable must be reconciled as the Germans reconciled it on their 20th of July 1944. Except that the Germans did the impossible too late. We, the French, will do it in time. This will be my historical mission: I shall lead the elites of freedom into the camp of Conservative power before nothingness overwhelms both freedom and power. Deep in conversation about the tactical steps to be taken in the following days, the poet and the General indulged each in his own dream. Toward eleven o'clock de Gaulle left and reached his country place at Colombey-les-Deux-Églises after midnight, on May 30 at 1:47 a.m.

very quiet the sound of the seine as it brushes against the pillars of the pont neuf. *a church clock near by struck half past eleven.* a railroad station: verneuil l'étang. through the open window of the railroad coach the voices of birds, like the sound of bells above enchanted ponds. *a few taxis went by lazily and not all the dromedaries had gone home yet.* lemonade stand bathed in white light among the black trunks of the tuileries gardens. *in the distance you could see the president of the republic dressed in diver's gear. he was accompanied by the king of greece, who seemed so young that one felt tempted to teach him how to read.* jacques tati, the comedian, opened the window of his apartment and fixed his shaving mirror so that the reflection of the round disk hit the cage of his canary on the floor below: the bird began to sing. the astral eyes of wols, the deceased tachist, inspected the japanese marten-hair brushes in santelier's shop on the corner of the rue bonaparte and the quai voltaire. *a young hetaera followed them and offered them her services.* a secretary of the president's opened a letter from the widow of audin, the mathematician who had been tortured to death. *it was raining gloves and a sharp november wind carried them away.*

"Pierre!"

"Yes?"

"I know what you're thinking."

"No, you haven't any idea."

"Yes, you think you are going to end it all."

"Okay then, you're right. But I don't like it when you creep into my thoughts, Solange."

"I can't stop thinking just because it doesn't suit you."

"But one should be able to stop thinking."

"You should say that!"

"Well, I'm not a strong thinker, am I?"

"You're intelligent and intense, Pierre."

"Thanks. I'm not in the mood right now to return your declaration of love."

"It wasn't a declaration of love. Just a statement of fact. I don't love you at all. Did I ever tell you I loved you?"

"No, but you like making love with me, or don't you?"

"I find you agreeable. You are tactful and intelligent and what I like about you is that you can't stop thinking. Not even in bed."

"Would you love me if at certain moments I did stop thinking?"

"Perhaps."

"I shall oblige in the future."

"Is that part of your program?"

"Are you planning to go on this way?"

"Yes, for just a few more minutes, if you don't mind."

"Why?"

"Because I don't like you when you're not intelligent, Pierre. You're not intelligent tonight."

"So you think Fayard is right?"

"There, you see how stupid you are? No, of course, Fayard is an opportunist. But escape, just because there are Fayards in the world?"

"All right, let's call it escape, though it's the wrong word for what I am going to do because I suddenly see the light."

"You mean, because you've suddenly developed a short circuit in your mind."

"Your sarcasm isn't very charming, Solange."

"I'm a Parisian. We don't talk the way they do at Bordeaux, those heroes of Gascony."

"All right, then, I shall talk as soberly as possible. I'll simply draw up an account for you . . ."

"Your program?"

"My conclusions. I'm going to ask you three questions . . ."

"I can't wait."

"Can one go with the Communists?"

"No."

"With de Gaulle?"

"No."

"With the Fayards?"

"No."

"Since there are just three possibilities, one must quit. That's what you call escape. It's my program. I don't escape. I simply quit."

"There is still another possibility."

"Which?"

"You could remain Pierre Grange. A man who thinks and says what he thinks."

"Say what I think? I can't even publish a list, produce a vital piece of information."

"It would be quite sufficient if you thought and spoke. To Fayard, for instance."

"Would I change anything by doing that?"

"No."

"Well then!"

"I am thinking of the Picasso anecdote that delighted you so. He said that if his pictures were packed into crates right after they were painted they would have the same effect they have exhibited on walls."

"All right. I shall put my thoughts into crates in the future. Although they are probably not as valuable as 'Guernica.' "

"Perhaps it might help if you told them to me?"

"That's exactly what I'm planning to do. On the beach at Lacanau you and I are going to pack my valuable thoughts into crates washed ashore by the sea."

"Where?"

"At Lacanau-Océan. It's north of Arcachon on the Atlantic."

"Ah, near Bordeaux. The defeated hero returning to his home in Gascony."

"Lacanau has the biggest dunes in France. At low tide the beach is one or two kilometers wide. You have to hurry if you are out and the tide comes in. And it's quite isolated in stretches. You'll be the brownest girl in Lacanau."

"It's no good."

"Why?"

"Because I can't come with you. I don't have the time. I still have work to do on the orders for Magnard and it'll take me at least till the middle of July."

"Couldn't you do that at Lacanau just as well?"

"I'm afraid I shan't be able to think of anything at Lacanau."

"That isn't the reason."

"You're right. It isn't the reason. I simply don't feel like watching you act the defeated lion licking his wounds. What do you think you are going to live on?"

"I shall ask my father for money."

"You've never done that before."

"But I shall now."

"Poor Pierre, you really are in bad shape. But I'm no good as a nurse. I love you when you are intelligent and intense, when you never stop thinking and saying what you think."

"So you do love me?"

"Did I say that?"

"Just now."

"I must have slipped. By the way, perhaps there is one reason why even I might want you to go to Lacanau. If it's true what Fayard says about the danger you're in, it would be good to go somewhere where no one suspects you. I'm a little worried about you, Pierre."

"Come along, let's go. They're turning off the lights."

"Yes, your German friend was right. They expect the police."

"I wonder if the police will dare thrash into the people here."

"They must if they want to clear the street. And they'll have their orders."

"It's an outrage. Oh, I could . . ."

"You'll have to drop the habit of feeling indignant. That doesn't go with your program. From now on you must want to be as deaf and empty as a shell on the beach of Lacanau."

"You're right. But if I don't succeed?"

"Take a return ticket, just in case."

"Charming, that Parisian cynicism of yours."

"Oh, heavens, can't you understand how glad I'd be if you came back?"

The people of St-Germain-des-Prés surrounded the cars honking "Al-gérie Fran-çaise," yet they did not raise a hand against the occupants, but began arguing with them, screaming and laughing. The Boulevard was flooded with people. I stood where the dark narrow Rue Dragon comes in and from here was able to watch the table where Pierre and Solange sat. I saw the lights extinguished at the Deux Magots and the Flores, at the Royal St. Germain, the Brasserie Lipp and the Calvet, and I thought, I hope Pierre and Solange won't sit there too long or they'll be in the front line later on. I was relieved to see them rise at last. It was a few minutes past midnight. At almost exactly the same time the Algerian must have left his place in front of the café by the Rue Monge. The café closed at midnight at the latest because there was nothing going on in this part of town any more at that hour. The patron must have simply kicked the fellow out at midnight unless

he went by himself. By then the Algerian had had enough
time to choose a suitable new spot. While Pierre and
Solange came toward me diagonally across the Boulevard
St-Germain, the Algerian must have crossed the empty
intersection of the Rue Monge and the Rue Cardinal-
Lemoine and stepped into the dark entrance of the butcher's shop right next to the entrance to the Metro station.
Whoever comes out of the Metro and aims for the Rue des
Boulangers must pass in front of this butcher's shop. I lost
sight of Pierre and Solange but a few minutes later they
reappeared. Pierre held Solange by the hand so as not to
lose her in the mob. It was a bit touching, for Solange
is not exactly the type of woman one must hold by the
hand. She has a sort of sporty elegance and makes quite a
lot of money with her textile designs for Magnard. But I
noticed the two let go their hands only reluctantly when
they finally stood beside me on the sidewalk. At this
moment the police arrived, a squad of at least three hundred men in large gray vans, in jeeps, with motorcycles
whizzing around. The motorcade stopped. In the sudden
silence one could hear the shattering of metal and glass
as a jeep ran into a van which had stopped short in front
of it. Jeers went up from the crowds on the sidewalk. The
brigade continued slowly, fanned out with clocklike pre-
cision over the Place St-Germain-des-Prés, rolled to a stop
and settled in the three side streets. The two last cars
stopped in the center of the intersection and released a
crowd of puppets in leather leggings and kepis who dispersed according to regulations, swirling their batons—the
famous meticulously performed attack of the French police. I caught just a blurred vision of them, for the entire
Boulevard had started to run in one hypnotizing move; I
was just able to prevent us from being swept away. Quickly
I pulled Pierre and Solange into the dark shaft of the Rue

Dragon. We ran down it a little way, stopped and looked back. Through the mouth of the lane opening into the Boulevard we could see the fleeing crowds but not the police. I figured that they had carried their attack no further than a hundred yards into the Boulevard. The concentrated movement within a small area would be sufficient to cause a centrifugal dispersing effect. "Sandbox games," I said to Pierre. "Observed with the cool Prussian eye," said a voice next to us. "Yes, but it's a Paris staff operation," I replied and held out my hand to Jacques Mondello, the philosopher. Mondello stood in the door of his little bookstore on the Rue Dragon. The store was dark, with only a small lamp under a green glass shade burning in the back. "Come in," Mondello said and we entered and sat down at the square table in front of the bookcases reaching up to the ceiling. Opposite the window I saw in the uncertain light the dirty-white wall of the publishing house where the writings of Vercors and Eluard had been illegally printed during the war and where the books of Samuel Beckett and Alain Robbe-Grillet and the now forbidden book of the tortured Henri Alleg were published. Mondello noticed at once what I had not sensed before in the Deux Magots: that Pierre was silent. They talked together for a while before unrest and fatigue drove us out again. Perhaps the young Algerian was the only person not restless and tired that night. Motionless he leaned in the shadowy black by the door of the butcher's shop near the entrance to the Metro and waited.

Before he fell asleep in his bed at Colombey-les-Deux-Églises the tall old General thought once more of the gate at the Élysée Palace, the gate reserved for heads of states only, which he had ordered opened because he believed in the power of ceremony, in the magic of rites, in the mes-

*merism of pantomime. Before the masses he would stretch
his long arms above his head in a great, solemn, slow gesture that made him seem even taller than he was. Let them
call me giraffe, he thought, the animal that stands high
above the veldt. He mused with satisfaction over the performance that had been put on for him: the ceremony of
the perfect coup d'état approaching in brilliant concentric
circles from the periphery toward its center, Paris, where
he, de Gaulle, stood motionless. He did not move a finger,
yet it was his coup d'état, worthy of his thoughts and ideas.
A coup d'état had its aesthetics too, which even opponents
admired although they might not use the metaphor of the
concentric circles but rather talk in terms of a noose that
had been put around the neck of the Republic. He would
not pull the noose. I am the rock of legitimacy, not the
hangman of freedom, he thought dramatically. Then, in
tactical terms: I shall send Trinquier and Thomazo to the
front so that I can ban Servan-Schreiber's paper when it
insults the army. I shall play like a juggler with the factions, the League and the Huguenots. I shall fuse the capitalist groups behind Mendès-France with those behind
Reynaud. Capital has but one honor: interest. I shall grab
it by its interest like a soldier by his honor. With some
uneasiness he thought of his own interests. His family's
capital was invested in Algerian banks. He knew that
money was the only power a king of France had to worry
about. But if this principle were altered other powers
would take the place of the power of money. The terror
of an ideology, for instance. That night General de Gaulle
did not know that perhaps at the same hour a great and
good man who had known nothing about the necessary
aesthetics of a coup d'état was receiving his death sentence
in Budapest.*

lacanau-océan: the waves, the heart-shaped shells, the sand crystals, the blowing wind. *it may not be absolutely clear today what one must fight for, but we know beyond any doubt whom we must fight. inevitably, and as of today.* the ultramarine blue of the sea and the bright gloss of the sky. whisky bottles and vases from atlantis thrown onto the beach, *to fight now or to fight later—that is the only alternative for those who cannot bow to orders of the legionnaires.* crab skeletons, death, veined pebbles, silence, paperlike rustling of waves, infinity. *the future begins today.*

"I admire your trust in what people have told you about democracy, Pierre. I'd have thought you more intelligent than that. The function of the public, is it? The purifying power of the press, eh? A deplorable fact is made public and before you know it is only half as deplorable. At least the person who made it public has cleared his conscience. He can go on to the next deplorable fact."

"Supposing Fayard published my list. That would have an effect, wouldn't it?"

"Yes, it might—it might, I say—force de Gaulle to issue a few statements. Your list and his statements—you and de Gaulle—would have added a few not very important pages to the volume of historical documents."

"Isn't there a chance, Mondello, that my list might be quite effective in warning the Republic? If it were proved that de Gaulle is a plotter . . ."

". . . the President of the Republic might be persuaded not to entrust de Gaulle with a new government. Is that what you mean?"

"It would be logical."

"And you in the part of David slaying Goliath."

"You can't deprive me of any more illusions tonight,

Mondello. But let's stay with the idea for a moment: all right, I am David. To all intents and purposes my sling-shot should be effective."

"Now I've got you where I want you. Do you know the difference between you and David?"

"Well?"

"David used a real slingshot, whereas you want to pub-lish an article which proves how evil Goliath is."

"But the article is my slingshot."

"That's where you are wrong. It's nothing but a piece of literature. This type of literature—newspaper litera-ture—has a certain justification as long as political powers are in balance. Or else when democracy is developing: Zola in the Dreyfus case. But when politics become the mere exercise of power it's all over. At that moment the press and its literature become a mere footnote to the premises of power. You, Pierre, are a victim of false doctrines about democracy. One of them is belief in the press and in the immediate effectiveness of literature. You have been told that freedom is identical with freedom of the press . . ."

"And you mean to say it isn't true?"

"It's an illusion to deceive trusting souls, leading them to write and read rather than to act even in the face of an opponent for whom words like freedom, writing and read-ing simply don't exist. Whatever needs doing is delegated to the press. Action really means that somewhere letters pour from a printing press."

"Thank you, Mondello, you've released me from my last inhibitions."

"Inhibitions about what?"

"I'm quitting. I've told Solange so earlier this evening."

"You mean you're going to bolt now, Pierre?"

"You yourself have convinced me that everything I've thought up to now is completely useless. Or is it?"

"But don't you see, I only want to make you think of something to do that may be of use?"

"There isn't anything. We live in a world of false alternatives. I can't go with any of the fighting factions. Not even with the lesser evil. To my mind the lesser evil is the greatest of all. I admit that till tonight I believed in a Third Force: the public. You've done away with that illusion."

"It's a neat calculation, Pierre, a trifle too neat."

"I can't help it if you don't like my conclusion."

"You simply wipe out everything that's left."

"What is left?"

"Evil! You've forgotten that injustice remains even if you quit. You can simply walk out, nobody will stop you— but don't forget, some Alleg will go on being tortured wherever you may be."

"Good God, Mondello, but that's why I go, because I can't do anything about injustice."

"Who says you can't? After all, you meet it everywhere. You have a special talent for running into brutality wherever you go. I ask you, Pierre Grange, why didn't you face up to Léon Delbecque in Algiers, pistol in hand? You're a reserve officer, you know how to handle arms."

"So that's what you are driving at!"

"Indeed. Instead of doing the obvious you made a list, and because nobody will publish it, your world collapses."

"Oh, I forgot. Jacques Mondello, the philosopher of direct action. Unfortunately, I don't believe in individual terror."

"Yes, you prefer to capitulate to the great universal terror."

"So you believe one must be able to kill when one encounters injustice?"

"Of course."

"Doesn't that just lengthen the chain of injustice?"

"Don't worry about injustice. It's here to stay, forever. But you may interrupt it occasionally, break the chain so it will take time to weld it together again."

"I'm afraid our conversation is becoming too abstract. I am talking about myself now: I believed in the power of words for a while. It was a mistake, I admit. But I cannot kill. Now you know why I am going away."

"And if you were taken into the cell where Alleg is being tortured—would you still be unable to shoot at his torturers?"

"Perhaps. I don't know."

"I respect your decision, Pierre. Perhaps it's good for you to go away for a while. To go away so as to realize that freedom doesn't mean being able to choose some ideology but to smash injustice wherever you meet it."

"And how do you recognize it?"

"Believe me, you recognize it always and at once. There's a sure sign: when nothing tells you any longer to write, when you are dominated by a single thought: to act, just to act. That's where you confront evil."

"But is there no chance for literature any more?"

"Not for the kind of literature you mean, Pierre— secondary literature that thinks itself history because it gets excited and argues. It is just a symptom, nothing more. Great literature does something else: it prepares long and gradual developments, it sows seeds, a few thoughts and forms which renew the world, which remind it of something old: Augustine did that, Pascal, Spinoza, Marx, Kafka—take his 'Knock at the Gate,' for instance, those few pages of prose don't influence the times but they change the world. A few things have become absurd since we have this story. . . ."

"It's late, Mondello, I must go. What books shall I take into my retreat?"

"None! But don't forget—I know, you'll think I'm quite ridiculous—still, don't forget to read the papers, Pierre."

After we had left Mondello we went back once more to the Place St-Germain-des-Prés where the police had formed cordons. They were relieved every half hour. Behind them the people of the quartier stood massed, watching the gendarmes silence the Gaullist horns by smashing the car windows with their batons. We stood around and met everybody. After two o'clock the muted demonstration crumbled away; the police had behaved with reserve, they had been wise and had waited. The Algerian was still standing in the entrance of the butcher's shop on the corner of the Rue des Boulangers. The passing of time faced him with a problem: Pierre Grange could no longer come by Metro but only on foot or by taxi. If he came by taxi, he would probably drive up to the house in the Rue des Boulangers where he lived; in that case the Algerian would have waited in vain, for he could not place himself in front of the house. Pierre would see him and would already have gone in before the taxi left. The Algerian could not make up his mind to change his position. We took a taxi and first dropped Solange at her apartment in the Rue d'Assas. Pierre and Solange kissed but Pierre did not go up with her. We drove along the Jardin du Luxembourg and the Rue des Écoles, which leads into the Rue Monge. At the intersection of the Rue Monge and the Rue Cardinal-Lemoine, Pierre knocked on the window of the cab and we got out. "I don't like to drive up to the house," Pierre said. He had an aversion for janitors and hated to be kept tabs on. We paid the driver. The taxi drove off and for a moment we stood in silence at the completely empty intersection.

Two seventeen. The tall old General slept. There is a very simple secret to the success of great old statesmen: they fall asleep easily. Anywhere and in any situation they are able to drop off into a deep refreshing nap. They sleep in cars, at diplomatic conferences and in their beds. The world is full of sleeping statesmen.

the whistling sounds of the morse code in the police radio car, like signals from the moon. from the direction of the comédie francaise a clearing of the throat, probably by racine. a dog peeing against the pedestal of diderot's monument. smell of violets.

Crossing the intersection, lit by bobbing electric lights but also by the moon, we made for the corner of the Rue des Boulangers. Against the gray fronts of the old houses the window cornices stood out black. When we passed the entrance to the Metro, I looked down the stairs and could read the white enamel signs on the doors saying "Poussez." I knew the doors were dark green. They must have been closed at this hour.

In his dream the General recalled a remark by Malraux. "The language of your speeches and memoirs is wonderful old classical French," Malraux had said. "Your style is the style of Montesquieu." Now Malraux repeated his words, and as the General dreamed a smile flitted across his face.

portillon automatique. the sweetish odor of the stairways. carnets for hades. the entrance in art nouveau style designed by guimet, iron vines. thundering trains across the styx, behind the portillon automatique.

At this moment the Algerian broke from his cover. He certainly had not counted on Pierre being in company,

but he had to risk the assault. It was lucky for Pierre I was
his guest this Night of the Giraffe. Perhaps I saw the Algerian a split second sooner than Pierre, I saw him the way
one sees a shadow, but what distinguished him from a
shadow was the dull gleam of an object which, as I pulled
Pierre aside, went into the sleeve of his coat, tearing the
material with a short crackling sound before it hit the flesh
of Pierre's arm.

*One of the General's dogs moaned in its sleep, woke up,
yawned and at once went to sleep again. The General's
hand slid down from the coverlet and for a time hung over
the edge of the bed, then rejoined the other hand on the
General's chest as if in prayer. The General always slept
as if he were lying in state—the King of France on a cata-
falque. But this was not Reims Cathedral yet.*

make up your mind! you can clench your fist, if only
inside your pocket, or you can try to widen the scope of
the human eye. rebellion, or adding a new kind of blue
to the spectrum—but make up your mind!

I believe the pain of the stiletto in Pierre's upper arm
was what saved him. It forced him into sharp and immediate consciousness, so that he grabbed the Algerian's wrist
with his right hand and bent it back; with his fist he
plucked the stiletto like a fruit from the Algerian's open
hand and thrust the knife into his chest in a move of automatic and blind force. The Algerian crumpled down on
his knees, then toppled backwards and collapsed on the
Metro steps. Sliding a bit further down, he lay still. We
ran down and gazed at him; he made no sound. His white,
broken eyes reflected the streetlights from the crossing.
Pierre pulled the knife from the body and threw it down

the steps; it clattered against the doors. Then we both hurried silently along the Rue des Boulangers to Pierre's house. As I dressed his arm upstairs in his apartment—he was bleeding heavily—I muttered: "That dirty little hired guy!" Pierre talked hardly at all, but toward morning when the dim light of a rainy day came creeping along the roofs of the Ile St-Louis outside his windows, he said: "My list wasn't worth that." His face was white and I knew as I looked at him that he would not return from Lacanau-Océan or from wherever he was going.

Around the World
the German Way

JOHANN BENEDIKT ZIMMERMANN received the first draft
order of his life in the year 1899 at Monastir. He was
twenty-two at the time and worked as a clerk and handy-
man for Monsieur Perrot, buyer for a Lyonnais wholesale
wine dealer. Vaguely turning over the note that had been
delivered to his room in the small hotel where he lived,
he glumly looked out on the street and up into the Balkan-
blue sky of the nineteenth century stretching above the
flat brick rooftops. The letter addressed to him by the
German embassy in Constantinople contained an unmis-
takable warning not to evade the draft any longer. Its tone
and wording were final. Johann Benedikt was furious. He

liked the Macedonian life, the view of the minarets, the pubs where you sat at small tables drinking dark yellow, heavy, oily wine with Serbs, Greeks and Bulgarians, the smell of roses and mutton fat that hung around in the alleys. When he thought of Madame Perrot, with whom he slept on the nights when his boss was away on business, he wondered whether it might not be better just to stay. Their affair had reached the point where the mere thought of her rustling underclothes and her sweet, ladylike face under the piled-up hair made him restless. Only much later his mind turned to Barbara; in those days Angélique Perrot's chemise was closer to him than the skirts of Barbara Weitz, of Kenzingen by the Kaiserstuhl Mountains, who was his fiancée.

He remained at Monastir to wait for Monsieur Perrot, who happened to be away on a trip. Three days later the elderly *grandseigneur* in his top hat and flowing overcoat emerged from the coach in which he had visited the wine growers in the vicinity. "Your emperor needs you," he said, squeezing Johann Benedikt's hand in sympathy. "Not against France, let us hope," he added pensively. He paused, and without batting an eye remarked casually: "Think of Madame when you think of France." Johann Benedikt's sunburnt face turned even darker and he bowed deeply to Angélique, who had put on some rouge.

The next day he took the train to Salonika and embarked for the Golden Horn. His decrepit old Turkish coastal steamer tied up at a pier on the Stamboul side, which meant that Johann Benedikt had to cross the Galata Bridge to Pera where the German embassy was. The bridge was a swirl of dust clouds and harsh, glittering sunlight; in the distance, the blurred minaret of the Sultan Ahmed Mosque pierced the sky. Innumerable children tore screaming through the hot yellow haze and clung begging

to the flaps of Johann Benedikt's heavy cloth jacket, under
which the gold watch-chain dangled across his vest. He
wore a bowler on his head; beads of perspiration welled
forth from under it and way down into his high, stiff collar.
He brandished his walking stick defensively, which only
seemed to double the commotion around him. Tired,
sweaty and hungry, he finally ducked into the maze of
alleys on the other side and after some search duly found
the embassy building. He was told to wait in a room
already peopled with some runaway German sailors,
tramps and shabby-looking adventurers, all of them people
obviously brought here by the Fatherland's search war-
rants and the smoke of guilt that rises from burnt draft
orders. Among them, in his correct clothes he looked a
strange sight. After hours of waiting, the voice of a medical
NCO finally wrenched him sharply and probably forever
from the daydreams in which he was deploring his obedi-
ence and wishing himself back in the pampered life with
silk-skinned Angélique. A long and harassing physical
examination began, but was called off abruptly in the
evening. A sentry was placed outside the door and they
were given to understand that they would spend the night
on the floor of the room. The food they were brought was
prepared in the Turkish way and inedible. In the morning
an officer appeared and finished up the examination.
"You'll make a good sailor," he told Johann Benedikt after
having had a good look at his tall, powerful figure. Johann
Benedikt thought for a moment of the cool vaults where
he had learned the cooper's trade and how it now would
take him two years longer to become a cellarman; but
then, giving in to the inevitable, he told himself that even
these two years would pass.

Those fit for service were assembled immediately in a
small platoon and marched off, escorted by the medical

NCO and two sailors. They were taken again across the Galata Bridge, again the children went wild, but this time Johann Benedikt was not upset, just felt slightly uncomfortable. They began to sing and tossed small coins to the children. Then a yawl took them aboard His Majesty's Ship *Loreley*, a stationary yacht in the service of the German ambassador to Turkey which was lying in the Constantinople roadstead. Johann Benedikt immediately found and gave money to the cook, who in turn came up with frankfurters and sauerkraut. Hidden away in the galley, Johann Benedikt greedily allayed his ravenous hunger. After finishing off with three bottles of strong beer, he went back to join the others and have himself fitted out. He carefully packed his civilian suit in the valise he had brought along, but could find no place for the bowler and the walking stick. In a sudden surge of temper he ran out on deck and with a swoop of his arm hurled them into the water. "I could have used that stuff," a mate who stood near by said ruefully. "Wish you'd given it to me." Side by side they watched the strange insignia of another life drift off on the dancing waves of the Bosphorus toward the Aegean, into the sunset.

Next day the drill began. Johann Benedikt was enrolled with the recruits who were to be shipped back for home duty on the *Loreley*'s next trip to Germany. Since for the time being there was no question of such a home voyage, they were drilled on board. Johann Benedikt most resented the part of the drill that bore the high-sounding name "seaman's training" but in actual fact consisted almost entirely of rowing. He chafed his buttocks cruelly on the hard benches and spent the rest of the day with a sore behind. Training at the *Loreley*'s small-caliber cannons was a relief, by comparison. That night he lingered dead tired on the edge of his bunk, staring into the dark recess of the crew's quarters. As he dozed, surrounded by the smoke of his pipe, he dimly realized that his body was far from turning hard and supple but felt just blunt and numb.

But he was lucky. Relief came only eight weeks later one day in the shape of an army physician who examined the recruits aboard the *Loreley* for fitness to serve in the tropics. When the examination was over—Johann Benedikt was, of course, also passed for duty in tropical latitudes—the yacht left Constantinople and took a southerly course through the Strait of Gallipoli. Rumor after rumor went around among the crew, until one morning they spotted the outline of the Greek coast through a delicate veil of morning haze. A flotilla of troopships swarming with soldiers and sailors was waiting for them at Piraeus and soon thereafter they put out to sea. The gay life on board, the feverish activity of a thousand men not knowing what was happening to them, subsided in the damp heat of the Suez Canal and the Red Sea. Slowly the ships pushed their way along the flat banks of the desert and past the whitish-gray, cubical houses of Ismailia and Aden, looking as though spotted from the plague. At last the Indian Ocean mixed a somewhat lighter blue into the simmering sea's liquid lead and brought a breeze of palm trees and vanilla. Now there could no longer be any doubt that it was the Chinese War which was drawing like a magnet these ten-thousand-tonners with their hulls stuffed with soldiers. Johann Benedikt sometimes wondered why throughout the voyage he kept his eyes fastened mostly on the eastern horizon, where one day Singapore appeared, or the coast of Sumatra, and seldom gave a backward glance to where he knew Europe was, Europe almost completely at peace for a hundred years, which he had been forced to leave for the shores of a junglelike, perilous, warring continent. One

gloomy evening in February of the year 1900 they sailed
into Kiaochow Bay where the East Asia cruiser squadron
was already anchored, ominously bright with its snow-
white paint and yellow superstructures.

They did not stay long at Tsingtao but were shipped to
the Taku Bar, where Lord Seymour was organizing the
international expeditionary corps. Johann Benedikt would
have liked to investigate the small villages and towns along
the mouth of the Pei-ho. The colorful uniforms of sailors
and soldiers from England, France, Germany, Russia,
America and Japan floated through a mud-colored sea of
curving roofs, lettered banners, inscrutable faces and lurking silence. But he was immediately detailed to a platoon
of the German sea battalion assigned to guard the Tient-
sin–Peking railroad, then just under construction, in so
far as it was in Allied hands. Every now and then they were
engaged with antiforeign troops, but on the whole the
Chinese seemed quiet and friendly people who received
them with courtesy, and whenever Johann Benedikt
wondered what he actually was doing in this country he
could find no satisfactory answer. Compared to the inhabit-
ants, of, say, the Balkans, who in his experience could not
even imagine an argument which did not end in a fist
fight or at knife's point, these placid rice farmers in their
sleek, long tunics were just the right partners for endless
diplomatic conferences, for sly games, talks and quiet
maneuvers such as Monsieur Perrot might have conducted.
There was something wrong in the way things were being
handled, Johann Benedikt thought.

At night they patrolled the railroad tracks in small
details to prevent acts of sabotage. One night they heard a
suspicious noise by the embankment in the distance. They
put their ears to the tracks and listened. Finally Johann
Benedikt and another soldier were sent forward to recon-

noiter in order that the entire patrol should not fall into a trap. The night was dark and fog rose damply from the fields. After a while they saw a man lying on the tracks. He was on his back, his arms thrown over his head, his hands clutching the ground. They bent over him. Just as Johann Benedikt noticed that the man's throat had been cut, he heard a hissing sound and a groan; before he could straighten up he received a terrible blow on the back of his head. He staggered back, saw his comrade collapse on top of the dead man, and facing him, like a shadow, the shape of a huge Chinese rearing back to deliver another blow. He had struck him with the blade of a powerful, old-fashioned sword, and in its dull metallic glint Johann Benedikt saw the wrinkles of a primeval head above the billowing folds of the wide peasant smock. But his bayonet, dangling free at his belt, was quicker than the old man's sword and with it Johann Benedikt hit him over his bare skull so hard that it split right down to the bridge of the nose. A wave of blood washed over his sailor's collar; and the sword of the giant, who seemed to embrace him in death, dropped to the ground behind his back. He fell with the old man on top of him, and this was Johann Benedikt's luck, for the heavy body now shielded him as the partisans started shooting from the dark. By then, however, his comrades had also reached the spot and were opening fire. Most of them were sharpshooters, able to aim within a second wherever a flash burst from the muzzle of one of the antiquated shotguns. Since the Chinese had not learned the trick of rolling over a few feet after each shot, the infantry men counted twenty-two dead in the bushes and nearby ditches at dawn when the ghostly show was over. They themselves had only one casualty, Johann Benedikt's companion who had been hit fair and square by the old man's sword. The second blow had slid off the thick, soft cloth of Johann Benedikt's blue sailor hat and flattened him out on the ground, thus enabling Johann Benedikt to get away with a bruise, if a large, swelling one. Gazing at the mighty form, they were struck by the old man's heavy, bloated breast and a certain softness that had come over the body in death. When they examined the corpse, they discovered that they were looking at a huge old woman. The sight of the giantess made them fall silent. As she lay there she seemed a thousand years old.

The affair had an unpleasant aftermath in that they were reprimanded for not having brought the saboteurs in alive, as an existing order prescribed. A collective charge against them was dropped, but a British army prosecutor picked on Johann Benedikt's "case," since it turned out that the old Chinese woman had been a famous and long-sought bandit leader. It was about this time that the expeditionary corps reassembled at the Taku Bar to prepare for the famous March on Peking. In this period of anxious waiting, the air became tense with national jealousies and international irritations. So it happened that Johann Benedikt one day found himself before a military court of inquiry, composed largely of Englishmen, which sentenced him to eighteen hours "at the wheel." This, of course, promptly set off a German protest. The second hearing took place before a mixed tribunal and a little Japanese lawyer was assigned to act as counsel for the defendant. He pleaded his case for three hours. Sitting quietly in the dock, Johann Benedikt gave monosyllabic answers to the questions he was asked. His broad, calm if not altogether good-natured face looked blankly at the uniforms of the high officers, who followed the hearing with keen interest. The sentence was mitigated to four hours of punishment. After it was pronounced, Johann Benedikt returned to the compound where the corps was billeted. A sullen mood of restiveness hung about the German quarters that night. When the British military police came for Johann Benedikt the next morning, they had to make their way through a stream of open threats. They led him to a gun that had been brought into position in the middle of the camp and strapped him to one of the wheels. There he stood, the world traveler in spite of himself, and looked into the faces of passers-by, who almost without exception felt embarrassed by the procedure or, if they were Germans, tightened their fists in their pockets. German officers came up to Johann Benedikt and made a point of engaging him in friendly conversation. The whole thing might not have been so bad, had he not found to his surprise that his thoughts kept returning to the old Chinese woman he had slain. During those hours her features carved themselves indelibly into his memory. She seemed to him like the primeval mother of all the Chinese race, a woman from an old legend whose slaughter meant some sort of sacrilege. That this should have happened to me of all people, Johann Benedikt thought. He felt almost gratified as the spokes of the wheel cut into his back, as though marking his atonement for a sin he could not quite understand. The world was becoming more and more of a puzzle to him.

He kept silent when a boisterous crowd of German sailors and soldiers surrounded him after the four hours at the wheel were over. They marched him in triumph directly to one of the largest teahouses in the neighborhood, a favorite hangout of the British mercenaries. They took over the place and grabbed all the girls who were still unattached. The atmosphere grew tense; the girls whispered excitedly and their kimonos rustled like paper. Then a short, stocky German sailor who had not been able to find a girl went up to one of the Britishers, a huge Scottish

Highlander, tapped him on the shoulder and grabbed the arm of the colorful little creature he was holding around the waist. The Scotsman swung back and planted his right fist in the sailor's face. That was the signal. German indignation over Johann Benedikt's humiliation burst forth in a wild roar of fury and the British, who were in the minority, were systematically pushed out of the teahouse. They put up a brave fight but in the end had to quit the field, covered with blood, followed by the Germans, who realized that military police would arrive any minute to make arrests. For a time the plaintive wail of a little Chinese lady, whose elaborate hairdo had suffered, hovered over the site of vanished lust, over the ravaged scene of thin china cups and soft clouds of rice powder which in more peaceful times would rise as a kind of incense.

The incident might have had unpleasant consequences had not their marching orders come through that very night. But within the British high command, resentment about the teahouse affair was deep and lasting, and the German soldiers and sailors grinned knowingly each time during those days of mounting misery that the order "The Germans to the front!" issued from Lord Seymour's tent. First Mate Petersen, Johann Benedikt's platoon leader, vented his indignation at such dubious favoritism in a barrage of abuse which always ended with: "Couldn't you dirty bastards have left the Tommies their girls?"

Laughing and cursing, they marched through China. But gradually the advance turned into a retreat, during which they were forced to form in squares to defend themselves against the onrushing hordes of guerrilla fighters. Instead of reaching Peking, they found themselves one day back on the coast, where there began a dull garrison life. In June they were ordered to take Fort Taku by storm, and once again an expedition was made into the interior. It went off somewhat more successfully than the first; this time, under the command of Count Waldersee, they actually got to Peking. On the whole, though, this was a quiet period. Johann Benedikt, meanwhile promoted to the rank of mate—for he was a good soldier, calm and tough— belonged to a small detachment which occupied the little town of Kianglin. There being nothing for them to do, he started an affair with a girl in Kianglin's only teahouse. When she found that tea made him depressed, she taught him to like the delicate, bitter rice liquor which is also served in teacups. But he was really pining for a bottle of Badensian wine, for a Kaiserstuhler or a Blauburgunder, grown on the western slopes of the Black Forest. He read with yearning the letters which Barbara sent regularly every month; they were written in a calm, steady spirit with only rarely an expression of impatience; he, in turn, wrote words of loving tenderness to Kenzingen and rejoiced as the year 1901 went by and the day of his discharge drew near.

And, in fact, one day early in 1902 embarkation orders came for large contingents of the German troops stationed in China. Johann Benedikt's unit was among them. With a feeling of vast relief he climbed the gangway onto the transport. Again they went to Singapore, but then, passing the Strait of Malacca, took a southwesterly course. "You'll be transferred to another vessel at Dar es Salaam," members of the crew explained. "We have orders to return to Kiaochow so the rest will get home sooner." They crossed the Indian Ocean, passed the Seychelles, and were glad to be offered a free glimpse of the Dark Continent. In the roadstead at Dar es Salaam a fleet of German ships was anchored, all of them flying the homeward-bound pennants. With two platoons of the first sea battalion Johann Benedikt boarded the cruiser *Habicht*. In the evening they

were given shore leave; they gaped at the exotic sight of
Bantu negroes and the beauty of the Indian women whose
bright-colored saris phosphoresced under the palm trees.
They slept on deck under the quivering heat of the African
night with the running lights softly bobbing from the
swell of the sea. They woke from strange dreams only after
they were well out to sea, and to their surprise found that
the ship's bow still pointed south. Johann Benedikt and
the others in charge were called before the captain and
detailed for duty. "Mate Zimmermann, you take magazine
number one," the executive officer said to Johann Benedikt. As they left the mess in a state of confusion, they
heard from the deck: "All hands man your battle stations!"
Johann Benedikt felt a tug at his sleeve. "Look up there,"
one of his fellows called out, pointing excitedly at the mast.
Then they all saw that H.M.S. *Habicht* had struck its
homeward-bound pennant.

They sailed for a long time and gradually circumnavi-
gated the Cape of Good Hope. The coast never came in
sight, but they guessed the route from the way the ship
took a more and more definitely northern course. The
journey seemed endless. Staring across the watery waste,
they were sunk in gloom. Whenever they asked the captain
or the officers where they were being taken, they were
answered with a shrug: the ship was proceeding under
sealed orders. Each morning, Johann Benedikt's bleary
eyes gazed into a merciless yellow sunrise like burning
red-hot sands; each evening, into the dark purple of the
rising night.

One night, after they had been at sea about two weeks,
a narrow, even coastline emerged from the waves far ahead.
The engines stopped and deep silence fell. "Lüderitzland,"
said an officer near Johann Benedikt by the rail, pointing
forward. There was nothing but this narrow coastal strip,

far over in the east where the night was moving in, nothing but the regular breathing of the swell from the vast ocean, nothing but the ship's sides standing steeply like cliffs at the entry of a continent, at a chasm of time. Rattling and clanking, the anchor went down.

That night rifles and ammunition were issued and crews assigned to the landing craft. As the dark faded away in the west, they saw that more ships had meanwhile anchored within sight of the coast. At precisely seven o'clock the boats were swung out and headed quickly for the flat shore, their oars whipping the water, the little black-white-and-red flags at the stern cracking in the wind. Standing in one of the dinghies with the men under his charge, Johann Benedikt kept his eyes fixed on the shore where a few houses began to appear. All of a sudden his mind went blank, as a swirl of shots whistled around them. He ducked down behind one of the rowing sailors, who suddenly let go of his oar and with a great sigh collapsed on the gunwale. One of the marines was hit by a bullet and fell overboard. Nearly all the boats spun about with their rudders left untended. In the silence that followed they heard triumphant cries from the shore. From the bottom of the boat Johann Benedikt cautiously reached for one of the oars; others followed his example and they got the boat under way again and back to the *Habicht*. They counted three dead and several wounded and Johann Benedikt started the Herero War with a shot that had grazed his lower left arm.

Toward noon the gunboats and the small cruiser moved closer to the shore and opened fire from their batteries. With their help a second attempt to land was successful. By evening they had dug the first field positions in the coastal sands of the Namib Desert. It was the first night in many weeks that Johann Benedikt no longer thought of a possible return home. Huddled behind the breastwork, he listened to the rumble of faraway thunder and watched flashes of lightning crash into the soil of Africa. It took until the autumn of 1903 to quell the revolt of the Bondelzwaarts, and when this had been achieved, Chief Samuel Maherero of Okahandja sent masses of his Herero against them. They had left the Namib Desert far behind and were now proceeding north through the bush. In the distance, herds of wildebeest whirled up clouds of sand from the Etosha Pan. All that year the fighting and marching continued until the battle at the Waterberg. Again came a wet season with damp heat and torrents of rain. The news of Maherero's death reached Johann Benedikt in a bout of fever, but still they were made to fight on against the hordes of savage Hendrik Witboois until 1905; mail no longer reached them in the bleak lava desert of the Naukluft Mountains, nor did Johann Benedikt hear anything from Barbara during all the following rainy season. He now wore a sou'wester, and a light-colored beard framed his emaciated face; once it had been broad and calm, now the eyes burned deep in their sockets. When he walked through one of the deserted villages he was seized with horror at the silence pervading the domed huts around the empty kraal. With a feeling like that when he gazed at the old partisan woman years ago in China, he now looked down at the bodies of the slain Herero; in death their filed teeth showed between gaping lips, while over their leather garments and iron jewelry the evening washed its sand-colored light.

In the end the Herero were rounded up to the last man in the Kras Mountains and by the Great Fish River. Colonel von Deimling's troops drove them from their springs, chased them with rapid-firing, long-range rifles from their last waterhole. They chose to die from thirst.

This may have been the reason Johann Benedikt's face never broadened into a smile, in spite of the joyous shouting that filled the air, when the returning colonial force marched down Hamburg's Jungfernstieg on a hot day in July of the year 1906. His thoughts were still back in the shade of a tamarisk tree, listening to the plaintive cries from the waterless sands of Omaheke where a black people was dying of thirst. He looked into the faces, peered down the street and was amazed to find that the world had not changed since 1899. Black-white-and-red flags were still flying from the houses, faces were still red and well fed, and women still gathered up their skirts daintily from the dust the way they had always done.

After he had mustered out and been discharged, he took the train to Kenzingen, where Barbara met him at the station. She had not grown younger either in those seven years, he noticed, but under the fine brown hair her face was still beautiful and good and he was most gratified to find that her caresses had grown twenty-five years old with her. They had a child within the first year of their marriage, a daughter, and a son in 1910. Johann Benedikt became cellar-master in a champagne cellar at Emmendingen. He tested wines and watched over the fermentation in the bottles. At certain intervals he got drunk. He never went home on these occasions but would stretch out in a field, let the stars revolve above his head and in his mind turn the nocturnal silhouette of the Kaiserstuhl into the outline of Fort Taku. Unconsciously he avoided talking in front of people. He became, on the contrary, more and more taciturn, and Barbara decided that she liked him even better than she had before, knowing as she now knew that he was not sullen but just discreet.

On Sundays they would sometimes go off with the children. They visited the cathedrals of Strassburg and Freiburg and looked across Alsace and the Upper Rhine from the Breisach Hill. Close at hand the grape leaves, poplars and bright-colored South German houses stood out clear and sharp against the delicate haze of the distant Vosges Mountains.

But above all Johann Benedikt liked to walk in the marshy woods along the banks of the Rhine, where mosquitoes sang in the heat and ivy coiled around the acacia trees. In that green wilderness, sitting on the bank of a little branch of the Rhine, he forgot all time, alternating between puffs from his pipe and whistling himself a tune.

So it was with Johann Benedikt Zimmermann when in August 1914 he was reached by the second draft order of his life.

The Crocodile

HERR SCHMITZ had ordered a "terrine du chef" as a first course for the chauffeur. "You like a soup to start with, don't you, Jeschke!" But to their surprise they were served cold cuts, smoked meat, sausage, and pâté de foie gras. Summoned by the doctor, the garçon had shrugged the shoulders of his tail coat and explained in deplorable German that this was indeed what they had ordered. "Terrine," Herr Schmitz growled, "I could've sworn that was soup!" None of the three spoke French, neither Herr Schmitz, nor the chauffeur or Doctor Honig. French was the great gap in the doctor's education, but when Herr Schmitz engaged him he had grandly remarked: "Won't be necessary. The French market is of no interest to us. They know textiles themselves. We won't make any pubblig relashens over there." (He had said "pubblig" and had pronounced "relations" with a guttural R.) Because Doctor Honig remembered this concession, he now felt at a disadvantage not to be able to help.

Jeschke, gaunt and swarthy, probably a dedicated potato eater, examined the platter glumly, but after a few samplings admitted that the liverwurst was excellent. This was so remarkable in view of his customary reticence that Herr Schmitz no longer held back but began fishing tidbits for himself from Jeschke's hors d'oeuvres. He also invited the doctor to pitch in, but Honig preferred to wait for his escargots and, until they arrived, to watch the two men eating. Rigidly erect, scraggy Jeschke, who would not open one button of his gray uniform and poked his fork into the cold cuts from above; and Herr Schmitz, wrapped in firm, healthy fat, who, lying halfway across his plate, managed to talk, almost incessantly and yet quite intelligently, and still to eat intently and with relish—by no means a fat man, he could not be reduced to that simple a formula, but a man who for many years had fed carefully and only on the very best, which, the doctor pondered, is quite different from a man who gorges himself. Incidentally, before they had entered the "Anne de Beaujeu" Herr Schmitz had asked the doctor whether it would embarrass him if the driver ate with them and Honig had replied, of course, it was quite an imposition but he would resign himself to it. Herr Schmitz could, or rather had to, be given ironic answers. He hated flat agreement—"I don't like yes-men around me"—and that was what made life with him bearable if somewhat strenuous.

After lunch they left Paris by the Porte d'Orléans in Herr Schmitz's three-point-two BMW. Doctor Honig sat

in front with the chauffeur and Herr Schmitz in the back,
alone. The car was upholstered in pale, lemon-colored
leather, and Paris outside, behind the carefully plastic-
sponged safety glass—Paris was *vergammelt,* old and de-
cayed, as Herr Schmitz remarked wistfully. Yesterday at
Versailles Herr Schmitz had nearly blown up when he saw
the condition of the château. "Now really," he had said,
"they can't let the thing get that *vergammelt.*" He referred
to the château of Versailles as "that thing." The doctor
had said something about delicate patina, but Herr
Schmitz would have none of it. "That is no patina," he
had retorted, "that's filth. If those people really want to preserve their history, they must preserve it the way Louis the
Fourteenth meant it to be, that is, new and sparkling as
if it had been built yesterday." The doctor had thought
of Herr Schmitz's sparkling textile factories at Krefeld
and had said "aha!" to himself. But although he found
Herr Schmitz's point of view so disarming that he could
not think of any suitable comment, he had still—for con-
tradiction there had to be—made a few remarks about
beauty and weathering, aesthetics and history. Herr
Schmitz had remained unbending. "If you like it the way
it is," he said, "it's just because you can't visualize the way
it looked when it was new." And then he had let fly: he
knew all about the technique of housepainting in the late
baroque. The doctor had been amazed.

Well, looks like this is going to be quite an outing,
Honig thought, as they left Paris behind. France seen
through the eyes of the *Wirtschaftswunder* boy who sat
there behind him—alone in the back of a shining black
car on pale lemon-colored seats, alone not only in the back
of the car but in general, surrounded by an indefinite air
of aloneness which he apparently found hard to bear, since
he had taken the doctor along for company on this ex-

tended weekend. Chiefly for that reason. "Come along," Herr Schmitz had said, "let's get away from the 'shop-keepers' for a while and have ourselves a few nice days." But Doctor Honig knew he had not been chosen as a companion because Herr Schmitz found him more likable than his other "chiefs of staff." The boss was quite happy living among what he called "shopkeepers." Yet, for touring castles and cathedrals, he would rather ask along the one member of his staff whom he paid for knowing about art. ("About form," the doctor would correct him when he brought in a Huegi poster and the boss approved it, saying "Well, art is what you know more about than I"; but he could not break Herr Schmitz of the habit of talking about art, just as he could not keep his colleagues, the "shop-keepers" and the chief engineers, from calling him *Kunst*-Honig.) No, Herr Schmitz found him neither more nor less likable than the other people on his staff. Herr Schmitz was alone and didn't like it. He did without friends, but he needed company. You did not have friends, you had servants, one for the car, the doctor thought, and one for art, and you trained them to talk back, for there could be no success in a world that said yes to everything you did and thought. If you were as successful as Herr Schmitz, you were condemned to sit in the back of your car alone.

Of course there was still the question why, under the circumstances, Herr Schmitz would not rather travel with a woman. That he did not travel with his wife was easy to understand. Herr Schmitz's wife was a spouse; it was with the greatest reluctance that she ever left her house with the fake Chippendale furniture. Stranger, though, was the fact that Herr Schmitz was not known to have girl friends. Every time Doctor Honig thought about this aspect of his boss's life he instinctively looked at his hands: they were short-fingered but delicately shaped and covered with pale, tender skin; they did not go with the well-fed, prosperous body of the man—or were they probosces, the feelers of his success? Only a scarcely perceptible hardness distinguished them from the hands of a woman.

Herr Schmitz had no complaints about Chartres Cathedral. But the doctor thought it was too bad that they had arrived half an hour too late; the October sky had turned gray and the great rose window had begun to lose its sparkle. Also, it had been icy cold since morning. The wind was almost unbearable and the doctor felt he was heading for a bad cold as he admired the figures on the Portail Royal. He was anxious to get back into the car, but Herr Schmitz was indefatigable; glowing with enthusiasm, he circled the wind-swept edifice.

The hotel at Tours, on the other hand, in spite of being listed as première classe, was so obviously *vergammelt* that Herr Schmitz fled at the sight of the gray, tattered muslin curtains and the smudged doilies in the rooms and made straight for the dining hall, a dining hallette really, an eating cabinet decorated in Touraine fashion and fitted with a shiny, glowing grill. They ate partridges chasseur. Herr Schmitz rejected the first wine the waiter recommended. It was a Loire wine, hard at the core, with sugar added later. But Herr Schmitz was not a naïve German tourist who could be offered that kind of a wine; he was the son of a man who had owned a few excellent vineyards on the Moselle. The waiter quickly realized he was not serving a parvenu and brought a light, dry Barsac—"cellar temperature, not on ice!" Herr Schmitz had ordered—which after a while began to glow softly inside of them. Again Herr Schmitz talked, almost incessantly and yet quite intelligently, this time about wines, about German and French wines. He knew all about wine growing, cultivation and pruning, about wine trade and wine labeling.

The doctor, enveloped in his advancing cold, hardly registered the voluminous facts Herr Schmitz spread before
him. And once again he was amazed, for he, Honig, was a
man who knew much about literature and art, about
public relations and advertising, but little about facts.
Herr Schmitz abruptly concluded his lecture with the
remark: "France is really the only place left where you
can travel."

"Well," the doctor said doubtfully, "how about Spain?"
It only needed a cue to launch Herr Schmitz on a lengthy
discourse. So he dealt with Spain for a while before he said:
"France is much more refined, more distinguished,
quieter." The doctor was surprised to note the genuine
concern in the boss's voice when he added: "If only they'll
keep it from getting more *vergammelt.*"

Jeschke, by the way, did not dine with them. The doctor
found out a few things about the way chauffeurs live in
Grand Hotels; they were given small but comfortable
rooms on an upper floor and ate fixed menus in rooms
especially reserved for them. Herr Schmitz judged the
quality of hotels by the reports Jeschke had to give him
about the quality of his food. "If Jeschke says his food
wasn't good, you may as well write off the hotel," he told
the doctor. "A hotel that saves on that end won't be any
good in other ways."

When they went upstairs toward eleven o'clock and said
good night before Herr Schmitz's room, the doctor saw
Jeschke through the half-open door—his uniform still
firmly buttoned all the way up—as he was about to lay
out Herr Schmitz's night things. In the morning Jeschke
paid the hotel bill. He carried Herr Schmitz's cash for the
journey in his wallet and dealt it out in the same sure and
silent way in which he drove the heavy BMW. Actually,
it's only I who am the servant, thought the doctor, tossing

about with his feverish head; Jeschke is altogether different—a valet who lives with his master. It is a case of
symbiosis, like the affinity between the plover and the
crocodile. You had to be very rich to be able to own a
valet and Herr Schmitz was indeed a rich man. He was
neither medium-rich like so many, nor super-rich like
some of the newly rich whose pictures you saw in the
illustrated papers. He was a very rich, a genuinely rich
man. He was a crocodile.

At breakfast the doctor had a stuffy head. He was quite
dazed with the fever from the cold and a sore throat, but
outside it was a brisk, sunny morning, and he felt better
as they went for a walk around Tours. The cathedral was
tall and slender, and the palaces near by sat quietly and
autumnally behind their old walls as nuns and gardeners
passed in and out of the courtyards. The Loire, wide and
sand-colored, flowed past the city. They left Tours and
drove to Chenonceaux. Herr Schmitz's comments on Chenonceaux were neither pro nor con. What interested him
most in the long hall looking out above the river Cher
was a tablet recording that wounded soldiers had been
nursed here in World War I. He found the hall highly
unsuitable as a hospital. Obviously, Herr Schmitz was able
to visualize a hall full of wounded soldiers, to hear the
moaning of the sick in this empty, unheated place. Doctor
Honig had to admit to himself that this memorial tablet
would not have caused him any deep thoughts if Herr
Schmitz had not elaborated on it. Too bad, he thought,
for he would have preferred to talk with him about Diane
de Poitiers, about whom he was excellently informed;
there were a few beautiful portraits of the Fontainebleau
school in the château.

Subsequently Amboise, then Chaumont, and for lunch
they were at Blois. At Amboise, Herr Schmitz had been

far more interested in Leonardo's house than in the castle high up on the rock; the models of Leonardo's machines inspired him to some expert commentary. In the courtyard of Chaumont, the doctor, irritable from the fever, asked if this kind of architecture might not be studied equally well in all the villas of the Rhineland; but this time Herr Schmitz did not hear the irony and gave to understand that he admired the style of the Loire even in its turn-of-the-century copies, which struck Honig as the more peculiar since on the whole the boss found fault everywhere. Particularly the château at Blois; it was again, of course, completely *vergammelt*—black with age and looking out glumly across the tiled roofs of the town and down upon the shallow, lazy, Chinese-yellow river. In the afternoon Jeschke drove them to Chambord and more châteaux. It had turned increasingly cold. An icy wind whistled across the Touraine, and each time the doctor clambered out of the pleasantly heated sedan to inspect yet another château he feared his cold might develop into pneumonia. He envied Jeschke who did not have to look at anything, but could stay with the car, have a cup of coffee or linger around the souvenir shops, whereas he, Honig, had to "do" one sight after another. Herr Schmitz was indefatigable, and indefatigably he divided the monuments of the French past into *vergammelt* and well preserved. He made mental calculations and, as the afternoon wore on, he grew more and more depressed, for the cost of the work he calculated would have to be done exceeded everything he had expected. The French without doubt had overtaxed themselves with buildings in their past.

At Chambord they nearly came to blows. The doctor was overcome with delight at the mannerism of the château's roof-scape; certain surrealist pictures sprang up before his mind's eye and merged into illustrations from the Duc de Berry's Book of Hours. Francis the First had scratched "Souvent Femme Varie" on a window. All this inspired Honig to plan a poster for Herr Schmitz's Krefeld rayon fabrics which he would discuss with Huegi in Switzerland immediately after his return. "Do you know what Chateaubriand said about the roofs of Chambord?" he asked Herr Schmitz.

The boss started from a gloomy study of some empty windows which had been boarded up with rough planks. "Well, what did he say?" he inquired.

" 'Chambord is like a woman whose hair is blown high by the wind,' " the doctor quoted, off the cuff, so to speak, for he had just read it in a folder.

"Piffle," Herr Schmitz said brusquely. "You'd better look at the state the château is in." The doctor sensed with alarm that a kind of personal antipathy against him, Honig, had crept into his boss's voice. "Two thousand workmen slaved steadily on this thing for twelve years," Herr Schmitz added. "France bled for this castle. Do you know that this king—what was his name again? . . ."

"Francis the First."

". . . that this fellow founded a special finance committee which pillaged the country so that this thing could be built?"

The doctor did not know, and Herr Schmitz growled: "That interests me more than what some of these literary guys and art historians come up with. Mannerism! They'd better see to it that the thing doesn't deteriorate like this."

Cheverny, shining in the dark on its well-kept lawns within a glowing, dark-red park, slightly reconciled him with the generally *vergammelt* condition of French history. *Vergammelt*, thought the doctor, as he sat wearily next to the chauffeur on the drive to Bourges, a slang expression with an ancient Germanic root, *gamla* meaning "old" in the Scandinavian languages. Why can't he simply let old things be old and *vergammelt,* the doctor thought bitterly, as he stared out into the fleeting dark, feverish again and his head numb. They had "done" two cathedrals and eleven châteaux since last night. The doctor giggled softly and nervously to himself. Carefully cultivating a pleasantly snobbish style in traveling, he would not have thought that this kind of thing could ever happen to him.

At the hotel at Bourges he immediately asked Herr Schmitz to be excused and went to bed, but although he took two aspirins he failed to fall asleep. The fever kept him in a state of numbed wakefulness. The room where he lay was large and dark even though he had pulled the curtains back, for the street outside in nocturnal Bourges was somber; only the red lozenge-shaped lantern of a tobacco bistro cast a faint reflection on the ceiling. Close to ten o'clock there was a knock at the door and Herr Schmitz came in to see how his companion was doing. "Now get yourself into a good sweat," he said, "and you'll be rid of it by morning!"

"I can never get myself to sweat," the doctor said. "I always start a fever, just a slight to middling fever that goes away again after a while."

"A real fever and then a real sweat would be better," said Herr Schmitz. He sighed and pulled up a chair. Apparently he still had something on his mind.

"I was out walking for an hour," he said.

"My God," said the doctor, "hadn't you had enough yet?"

Herr Schmitz ignored the question. "I saw the palace of a man named Jacques Coeur," he reported. "It stood out quite clearly despite the dark. I looked it up in the guidebook. Jacques Coeur was treasurer to Charles the Seventh, the fellow put on the throne by Saint Joan. Right?"

The doctor nodded. "Jacques Coeur was a tycoon. He

got Charles the Seventh the money for his wars against England."

"You see," Herr Schmitz said, "it helps to know that Saint Joan was financed by somebody. That doesn't diminish her in any way. But somebody had to put up the money for the idea. There always have to be people who put up money for ideas to become reality."

He produced the platitude as if he had just made the most colossal discovery. The doctor would have liked to laugh, but there was something leaden, something suddenly sad about this heavy man sitting there by his bed in a dark hotel room in Bourges. Herr Schmitz slumped there like a sack and the doctor did not laugh, but he decided to use the moment to get his own back for the two cathedrals and eleven châteaux.

"And for what sort of ideas do you put up money?" he asked sharply.

But he had underestimated Herr Schmitz. The sack shrugged, but he had an answer.

"You show me a Saint Joan," he said, "and I'll finance her."

In the morning the doctor was a little better. The streets of Bourges were flooded with little girls in black school smocks. Cutting through the warm, living, yelling and whispering stream, the two men walked toward the cathedral which rested in the city like a giant, *vergammelt* elephant gone down on its knees. In fact, the cathedral of Bourges was the most *vergammelt* thing they had come across on their entire trip, but the doctor could not bear to have Herr Schmitz say so, for the cathedral was too enchanting in its decay. It was too magnificent in its elephantine fatigue for a capitalist, a *Wirtschaftswunder* boy, a textile manufacturer and Krefeld crocodile to need to worry about. Remembering his duty to contradict, the doctor asked Herr Schmitz why he would not simply admire the monument.

"Now listen," his employer said with surprise, "that's what I'm doing. Still, you mustn't make too much of what you love."

Only then did the doctor understand. As they entered the church he grimly recalled how Herr Schmitz had run down everything they had seen between Paris and Bourges. And why? Because he could not bear that the things he loved had become old and filthy, were withering away in neglected parks, staring from empty windows, dark, cracked and crumbling, and silently disintegrated with no sparkle from Krefeld factories to reach or brighten them. And suddenly the doctor knew Herr Schmitz's dream: sparkling factories and sparkling châteaux, a phantasmagoria of gleaming German factories and brand-new French cathedrals, a tapestry where past and present were interwoven in shining rayon threads, gleaming and made for all eternity: Krefeld and Versailles.

But there was no Saint Joan any more. Nowhere was there the slightest scrap of a myth Herr Schmitz might finance. Herr Schmitz did not see the glow in the painted windows of Bourges. His glance clung to the dusty tomb of Jacques Coeur.

When they left the cathedral the car was ready and waiting, reflecting one's image in its glossy black varnish, a coffin lined with pale lemon-colored leather. Jeschke had shined it to perfection.

Three Phases

SOME BEER had been spilled; it was forming a stain on the dark-brown table top. I took care that the *Rote Fahne* I was reading should not get wet. "Paulanerbräu," it said on the walls. / Now the second barbed-wire stockade was almost finished too, and tomorrow the striped prison outfits would be issued. / Some had been working as much as two weeks in the war cemetery; by some bad luck they had not been assigned for transfer to other camps. / The comrades were sitting on the pub chairs, talking to each other in hushed tones. They were straining for sounds from the street. / This evening during roll call it was announced that a penal company had been assembled; my name was among those who had been assigned to it. / All through that day I was being questioned I kept hoping there would be a transport tomorrow so I would be spared the cemetery. / I did not like the beer stains; they didn't fit in with the clean volumes of Lenin and Upton Sinclair I used to buy each month when I had made a little money. It was depressing to sit here and wait. / SS-Man Waldbauer came to the hut after roll call. He thought things wouldn't be so bad after all and again collected the letters he secretly mailed for us. / We were to be taken to Naples. The sea was glittering in the heat and we saw ships, but they were not the troop transports meant for us. / Heini Sauerland, who was the political chairman of the Communist Party at Neuhausen in those days and a member of the District Committee, had stopped playing "Roter Wedding" on the piano. With his half-blind eyes he was reading a document; he held it close up to his face. The light was dim in the Volkartshof pub. / At that time Willi Franz had not yet hung himself in his cell, but he already played chess so badly that I had no trouble beating him. We used to put the board on a tree stump outside the hut. / If you worked in the cemetery you were guarded by Negroes, we were told by those who had been there. / Most of the comrades were shabbily dressed but they had good heads and each one of them was a character. I had just gotten through Lenin's *Materialism and Empiriocriticism*; everything was quite clear: movement, too, was nothing but matter, and there was no God. Only the beer stains and the dreary waiting would not fit in. / Two hours ago a transport of a hundred Jews had arrived in the camp from Nuremberg; they were just getting settled in their hut. / The night before, German planes had made a raid on Anzio. All around the camp the lights had gone out; we had all been flat on the ground, with blankets tied around our heads to protect us against flying metal. Nothing had happened, though. / Each time the door opened, a gust of cold air swept into the barroom. In those days, the early winter of 1932–33, we were practically underground already.

That morning they had cut off our hair. This gave a boost to the pessimists who claimed we would spend a long time in the camp. One young Jew did not get his hair cut all over but had three strips shaven through his thick black mop, from his forehead to the nape of his neck. We looked at our bald heads and went around kidding each other. We still had not quite grasped the situation. / Next morning the convoys actually started moving. We left the cages and boarded trucks that were waiting outside the camp. The drivers of the trucks were Negroes. They lowered the backboards and shouted "Come on." Unwillingly we climbed aboard and huddled closely together. Two Negro guards climbed up with us, sat down on the backboards which had been raised again, and put their rifles across their knees. Then the trucks started off. / That night we were waiting for a parade the SA had announced. As for us, we had long ceased to demonstrate. The brief, illegal shock demonstrations of the Young Communists had been banned as "sectarian" by the Central Committee. At these activities the young comrades had been summoned by secret order to a party meeting-place. Upon a signal we formed a column and marched through a few streets in the workers' district. / After our hair had been shaved off, SS-Man Steinbrenner made us goose-step past a group of his superiors. At noon there was a rumor in the huts that Hans Beimler had been brought into the camp and had immediately been put into solitary confinement in a blackout cell. He was the head of the Bavarian Communist Party. We were all agog. / Even in the morning the sun was hot and glaring. The roads were bumpy and the countryside was completely devastated. At the entrance to the cemetery a large number of Negro soldiers was waiting for us. Spades, shovels and pickaxes were distributed under the supervision of a white officer. / We were carrying the red flag and shouted slogans such as "Workers, fight the emergency regulations!" "Join the KPD, the working-class party!" and "Down with the Hitler Fascists!" After about ten minutes we heard the sirens of the police flying squads in the distance and dispersed in all directions. Such activities were no longer under discussion by the time we met at the Volkartshof. We just sat around and ordered beer to make it worth while for the innkeeper. If the SA attacked us we would fight. But only a very few of us had ever really fought, I mean physically. I was talking to Schmeller, a student of music, about Hegelian dialectics. The formula—thesis, antithesis, synthesis—was quite easy to grasp. All you had to do was bring in the example of the egg. The bursting of the eggshell was the armed uprising. But I had a dim feeling that the whole thing was too simple. / Nobody had a very clear idea as to what the words "penal company" might mean. In the morning we were to be transferred to a hut that had no bunks, which meant that we would sleep on our pallets on the concrete floor. And that in April. However, that wasn't going to worry us. Every member of the penal company was soon surrounded by a certain aura. We felt part of an elite. The sky above the camp was still bright. Over where the sun was setting should be Dachau. / We were divided into labor details and scattered in small units over the country-side. Above the cemetery hung the sweetish odor of corpses. We started digging graves. The chalky soil was dry and hard. It crumbled in clods from the gleaming, silvery spades. / All of a sudden I felt quite certain we would never again gather so calmly in the barroom of the Volkartshof with its Paulanerbräu posters on the walls. Never again would Sauerland explain the Central Committee's latest resolutions, nor would the functionaries who were able to speak well rise and take the floor one by one. At the street counter, children were getting pitchers of beer for supper. As the dry, cold winter wind swept around the corners of the workers' houses outside, I was reading the news of death and loneliness in the puddles of spilled beer. Yet I still waited for a messenger to call out in a loud voice that things were coming to a head now. / The Jews would not stay long, we thought. They were all businessmen and doctors and lawyers. They could not possibly remain with us. Up till now only we Communists had been in the camp. The Jews were looking out of the windows of their hut. They were quiet and wore good clothes. At six o'clock two of them were called out to carry water. Steinbrenner walked into the compound shouting, "Goldstein! Binswanger!" They were made to grab a water barrel and follow Steinbrenner out of the gate. / In the cruel heat of the day water was passed around in cans, but it tasted of the chlorine it had been disinfected with, the same chlorine the corpses had been dusted with; it was revolting and you put the cup down after the first few gulps. Whenever we paused in our work and looked up, we saw the wooden crosses in huge square patches all around. After we had dug a row of graves we were taken off to fill the bags.

At that moment we heard the clatter of hurried footsteps outside and then the door flew open and Bertsch appeared. We started up, for the face of tall Hans Bertsch was covered with blood. "The SA!" he yelled. He had been wounded in the head and blood was streaming down his shabby gray overcoat. Bischoff, who had had a lot of beer—

he was said to be the head of the illegal Communist militia—roared: "Everybody follow me!" Some pulled steel rods and knuckle-dusters from their jackets and pushed into the street with him. Meanwhile Bertsch was leaning heavily on the counter. His face was chalk-white and red with blood, a metal worker, on relief for the last two years, and the pub was dark, dimly lit, a Munich worker's pub, cell meeting-place of the KPD, with beer stains on the tables. Before we rushed to Bertsch's assistance his glance went through us and broke against the windows, beyond which the dusk was winding its way through the streets of the years.

That night for the first time we heard shots that were meant for us. We were all standing by the wall where Goldstein and Binswanger were shot. The crackling volley caught us as we sat in the hut eating our evening soup. It silenced our talk, but we finished the soup. Only the Jews stopped eating; they were not as starved yet as we were. Goldstein and Binswanger never came back, although we waited and now and again asked for them in hushed voices. Next morning we stood lined up in a square. The SS-men wore long, gray coats like statues in the dark fog of April and a voice said across our heads: "Shot while trying to escape!"

We were given rubber gloves and high rubber boots to prevent us from getting infected. We took long white linen bags from a pile and flung them over our shoulders. In an open space in the middle of the cemetery the corpses were lined up in long rows. In the distance they just looked like shapeless clumps dusted with chlorine. The dead from the battlefield at Nettuno were being collected in this cemetery. Many of them had been lying about for several weeks. They had turned a bluish black and started to decompose. They stank. The ones that had not been dead for so long still showed somewhat lighter skin on their faces and under their ragged clothes. Some had no arms or legs or even heads, because they had been in the crossfire of the artillery from ships and shore. Flies were gathering around them in blackish clusters. The climbing sun loosened their rigor mortis and made the bodies soft and gelatinous. Black juice came oozing from them. We stuffed the spongelike lumps into the bags and soldered the wire at the tops. Then we took them on stretchers to the graves and flung them into the holes. They hit the bottom with a smack.

The Last Ones
at "Schwarzer Mann"

KARL ROLAND, the smuggler, formerly student of philosophy at the University of Königsberg in East Prussia until drafted into the infantry in 1939, stumped along the furrowed trail leading from Brandscheid village across the broom-covered slopes up into the forest. He knew that Lisa was following him with her eyes from her uncle's house where she was visiting, but he did not turn around.

"No, I won't come with you," she had said when he asked her, "it's too spooky up there."

It was going on eight o'clock of a July evening and over on the other side of the Belgian border the sky was a huge shield of gold. Roland crossed the Bleialf-Prüm highway at a dogtrot, and turned into a narrow lane not marked by any sign.

His tongue still tasted that abominable schnapps he had been served at the Brandscheid inn, where he had disposed of his coffee. A filthy, dark inn it was, and of course, they gypped him this close to the border. He surely would get more if he went further upcountry.

"What d'you do up there all the time?" the innkeeper had asked him suspiciously, pointing with his thumb to the ceiling of the bar as though he meant it rather than the woods up on the ridge of the Schnee Eifel. "Eerie place, huh!" and he spilled some of the schnapps he was pouring.

"I feel safe up there," Roland had replied and looked at the innkeeper. He knew they didn't like his look; they couldn't take it, and wished him to hell as soon as he had finished his business. His look came from far away, from a distance they could not even imagine.

"What d'you do with yourself in that terrible forest all the time?" Lisa also wanted to know. She wore a light summer dress in a large flowery print as she pushed her baby carriage through the village. She had real style, with her splendid ladylike face and dark hair; a treat for a man condemned to a life in the Eifel.

"I live there," Roland would reply quite truthfully as he walked with her through the broom or down a lane between the fields. "I live in a bunker," he explained to her. "They were all blown up but some casemates make good enough living quarters. I've a cot in there and a table and shelves for my stuff. There are even two pictures on the wall—a view of Königsberg and a picture of Rita Hayworth that I found in an old copy of *Life*. It's quite a snug place, really. And people can't find me up there."

The narrow lane emerged from a plantation of young

trees. Then the forest began. The pines stood darkly against the horizon and in front stretched a plain with battered stumps of trees. Each time he passed here Roland again heard the burst of the shells that had felled them. From the ridge beyond, a view opened across an ocean of flat valleys and forests crowding in from the west, from St-Vith and Malmédy. A rather geographical feeling. Roland loved borders where countries became uncertain, lost themselves in the woods, frazzled out in wagon trails which suddenly ceased to exist, in wheel marks, footpaths, under high yellow grass which no one ever cut, in swamps, slopes of waste land, junipers, ill-starred farms, loneliness, treachery and cries of buzzards. Schnee Eifel they called it, Ardennes, Hohe Venn . . .

It grew darker but there was still enough light to see by. Stumps of dead trees everywhere, and along the road concrete slabs of blasted bunkers sticking up into the air, pale like bone . . . it really was no place for Lisa, Roland thought. She would be scared. As a matter of fact, she only walked with him in the daytime. At the first shadows she would leave him on some excuse or other. He knew she was afraid. They were all afraid of him. Even the priest at Brandscheid was afraid of him, although Roland had told him the truth.

Tonight he had no plans. Anyway, the smuggling business was beginning to bore him. He knew the way via Ormont to the inn at Losheim by heart. At Losheim on the Belgium side he would stuff his rucksack full of coffee and push off to Brandscheid or Hallschlag, Winterspelt or Kronenburg, where he traded it for such a lot that he could take it easy again for the next couple of weeks. He still loved to eat and had gotten in the habit of drinking a little. So he bought some canned delicacies and, thinking also of Mike, asked the trader at Kronenburg to get him some whisky and gin. The Reverend Father at Brandscheid ordered books for him, new publications mostly, which Roland had read about in the papers.

But actually he was sick and tired of it all. The whole thing bored him because there wasn't the slightest risk to it. He would appear in the villages like a shadow. The border police had long given up trying to catch him. They knew he vanished somewhere in the Schnee Eifel, but the area was too big and not a regular base for smugglers. Nobody knew where there might still be land mines. And even the police found it just too eerie up there.

What if Lisa discovered there really was nothing dangerous about him, Roland thought. He would be quite embarrassed if she ever took his advances seriously. As far as he was concerned she did not have to fear for her marriage. He had only hoped that she might come up there with him just once and then try to help him. Didn't those old legends say that a girl's pure love could redeem a restless spirit? A romantic idea. She wasn't a virgin anyhow. Oh well, she'd be leaving soon. Too bad. Should he tell her what was wrong with him before she went? Nonsense. When the Reverend Father of Brandscheid would not even believe it.

The lane approached the stretch of forest called "Schwarzer Mann." From here it was two hours south to Brandscheid and two hours north to the gamekeeper's lodge at Schneifel. No human habitation in between. In the semidarkness the bunkers loomed up in ever more gigantic shapes, and here and there among the stumps the skeletons of trees stood out in pale relief. The last light was reflected in the deep puddles along the trail. A cross with a steel helmet dangling on it read "Unknown Soldier." Roland knew it could be only from his unit, and his mind went over the list each time he passed the cross.

There was a sound of steps and he saw Mike detach him-self from the dusk and head toward him.

"Hello, Charlie!" Mike said casually. "Got everything?"

"Uhuh," Roland replied. "Brought some whisky too."

He really went only for Mike's sake these days. Mike had learned to speak German quite well in the five years since February 1945; still, his American accent would have made him conspicuous had he ventured into the villages. He had belonged to the combat team of Bradley's army which held Schwarzer Mann throughout the entire Rundstedt cam-paign.

"Fine!" Mike said. "Get anything else done?"

Roland shook his head. He thought of his talk with the priest at Brandscheid. "Redeem us, Father," he had begged the reverend gentleman as he did each time he went to see him. But the priest became furious whenever Roland so much as touched on the subject. "You're crazy, man," he had said. "Leave me alone with those hallucinations of yours!" and added with a grunt: "All of you who spend too much time up there simply crack up."

"Why don't you report the case to higher authorities?" Roland had urged him. "Couldn't you put in a plea with the Archbishopric in Trier?" As usual, the priest had brushed it aside. "It's no business of mine. I say three Our Fathers for you after each Mass. That's all I can do for you."

With this the Reverend Father of Brandscheid had washed his hands of the whole business. He was an elderly gentleman and he figured, not unjustly, that he would be retired at once if he took Roland's story to Trier. But he too had been afraid. Roland had seen the fear flicker in his eyes.

He felt Mike's despair. Together they left the road and picked their way across the swamp. The bomb holes stood full of water. Cotton grass grew on the rims, giving a phosphorescent light in the darkness. The sign saying "Caution—Mines" and the French word "Danger" had long ago fallen over and disintegrated in the putrid ground. They made for the black wall of the forest across the plain of dead trees. Above them the sky was leaden. Clouds moving over from Belgium had pushed across the face of the moon.

Among the pines on the edge of the forest they came upon the first skeleton. From the mossy ground the skull gleamed dimly up at them. The uniform had disintegrated completely. Roland knelt down and fumbled for the Iron Cross which had all but rusted away long ago. Underneath the skull he found the paybook wrapped in oilcloth and thumbed through it. He had folded it into the cloth himself so the dead soldier could be identified when he was found. He snapped on his flashlight and for the thousandth time gazed at his own face. That was how he had looked twelve years ago. "Karl Roland," it said underneath. "Occupation: student."

He switched the light off and got up. Beside him Mike stood silent and glum, staring into the dark of the pines. In there was Mike.

"So he still won't have us buried?" Mike asked morosely. Roland shrugged his shoulders. "He obviously thinks we're harmless lunatics," he replied. "And perhaps he is afraid. I'm sure he is afraid."

When they reached the bunker he said to Mike: "They just don't believe in spirits any more."

That night, like almost every night, they played blackjack for a few hours and drank whisky in small sips before they went to bed.

Remorse

He had gone through the Confiteor, the Introit, the
Gloria, the Epistle, the Gospel and the Creed. Now came
the main part of the Mass. He bowed toward the altar,
kissed the stone, turned, and with his hands slightly raised,
said the *Dominus vobiscum.*

He watched them sit down. Even though he had been
celebrating Mass for ten years, he still was unable to tell
one face from another. They blurred before his eyes. Why
can't I ever focus on people, he wondered, now I have
gotten used to them? Used to them? That's a joke. Isn't it
they who had to get used to me? To the smooth, self-
assured routine I use in order to keep them at a safe dis-

tance? Yet, I cannot tell people apart. Seems to be some sort of stage fright still. He heard the server's *"Et cum spirito tuo."*

"Oremus," he added hastily. The church, the only one in town to have remained completely intact, swallowed the word smoothly into its mundane baroque. Pearly gray, shot with altar-gold and streaked with black shadows, it nestled egglike around his call for prayer. I should have said this outside, he thought, outside among the ruins. Ever since yesterday I cannot bear this church. Come to think of it, it has been on my nerves all along. Only I never knew why. I shall apply for a transfer to some poor parish. My superiors won't understand. But how can I go on belonging to the Chapter after this man has shaken my security? Not my faith, but my conscience.

He hoped to be able to lose himself in the prayer of offering as he took the veil from the chalice and raised the paten with the host. But habit left his face without expression. I must have said Mass two thousand times, he figured. It's a miracle I'm not thinking of the same things today that I still thought of yesterday during the sacred act. Today I think only of him. Yesterday, he reflected, I still thought of the article Father Eugene of the Jesuits wants me to do for his periodical, of the report about the clergy conference for the Cardinal, of the politicians who come to see me, hoping I might let them in on some secrets from the Archbishop's Office. I even thought of the superb lunch at Prelate Maier's to which I am invited every Saturday. Yesterday was a Saturday. But today I think only of this man who came to see me yesterday afternoon.

He walked over to the lectern side of the altar, and poured wine into the chalice the server held out for him. His lips murmured the formula: "Lord, who in a wonderful manner created and ennobled human nature and still more wonderfully renewed it . . ." while he added a drop of water to the wine. Secure in his vestments he went smoothly back before the altar, made the sign of the cross with the chalice and placed it on the corporal.

Not far from the church the little girl was playing among the ruins of a bombed building. She could not see the Sunday-quiet streets, for she had climbed across the bricks and rubble and was sitting in a little level patch she had cleared for herself a few days before. This is a nice place for playing, she thought, nobody will bother me here. I'm going to play going-for-a-ride with my wooden cart. In Bunzlau we always used to go for rides. But only with Mutti. Pappi was in the army and never around. I want to go for a ride with Pappi. I must hitch a horse to the cart. Maybe I will just take a brick; that makes a nice fat horse. It's a good thing Ulli can't see me here, she'd make fun of me. "How can a brick be a horse!" There is a piece of mortar that looks like a man. That'll be Pappi. I'll make it sit in the cart. Here we go, now. Giddy-up, pull that cart! The brick's too big, I can't take hold of it. I must find a smaller one. There, that one is just right. Now you'll be hitched to the cart. You'll have to pull Pappi and me. Where shall we go first? To the pile over there, that'll be the Riesengebirge. Pappi always tells me about the Riesengebirge. That's where Rübezahl the giant lives. I hope there is no Rübezahl. Pappi will keep him from hurting me. The small brick works nicely. I should have taken some string to tie it to the shaft. One of the wheels doesn't turn the way it should. Too bad Mutti isn't here so she can go with us. How that tree rustles over there! I hope there isn't a ghost in it!

"I struck my little daughter," the man with the bewildered look in his eyes had said to him. "I struck her in the face, very hard. I've come to confess. But I feel there is no forgiveness for a thing like this." He first seemed to me like one of those gentle lunatics we attract sometimes, the priest thought, holding his fingers over the Lavabo dish and letting the server pour water on them from the cruet. "I shall wash my hands with the innocent," his lips whispered. They were still without expression, but his eyes had begun to shine because they were gazing into that other face he had beheld yesterday. He heard the father say: "Oh, you should have seen the shattered look in her face. She did not even cry. You must understand, I had never hit her before."

Suddenly he realized he was saying the words about the "men of blood" which precedes the offering to the Holy Trinity. Weren't men like that everywhere? Weren't they in his church today, people with no remorse in their hearts, pouring from the ruined houses all around, hustling along the battered streets into the gold and gray of the egglike interior? What kind of people were they who filled the church? Murderers who had strewn bombs; women who were worse than whores—they did not even sell themselves, they were simply unfaithful; rich people who knew their riches were crime; priests who offered the sacraments as a matter of course: the sacred body distributed by habit among recipients who no longer questioned. But here I go scorning people, he checked himself. Many among them are driven to the Lord's table again and again by genuine desire. But when have I ever come across anyone who, like this man, blamed himself for an unforgivable sin? "Perhaps your little daughter did something bad?" he had finally replied. "And even if you really had done her wrong? I can see that you repent. Why shouldn't you be forgiven?"

"The Church forgives the great crimes," came the answer. "But how unimportant that is. It's the small deeds that destroy a man's life. Here, listen to me!"

Those words, "Pray, my brothers," which he had intoned to the congregation, tore him from his thoughts, but the subsequent long prayer of thanksgiving from the Preface and the beginning of the Canon gave him time to resume his reverie. The Canon contained all things created and all human concern. Also this man's concern, his urgent whispers?

There, now we have come to the Riesengebirge. I must build a church. That is the Abbey of Grüssau where I always went with Mutti. Pappi never goes anywhere with me. But it's not his fault, it's because there aren't any carts and horses any more. Grüssau Abbey, that was a beautiful church. Here they aren't so beautiful. All bombed. I went there once with Mutti. The organ was playing, as loud as anything. Up front stood the priest and his gown was like gold. A boy in a white dress held out a cup to him. I asked what was in the cup. Wine, Mutti said. Does he drink the wine? I asked. No, Mutti said, he transforms it into the blood of our Lord Jesus. But there's no such thing as making blood from wine, is there? We didn't stay long in the church. Later we drove on into the mountains for a bit. There was Rübezahl in the forest. I hope it's not going to rain. More and more clouds have come. I must put a raincoat on Pappi. Those leaves from the tree over there might do. But first I must build the church. For the towers I'll take rocks that are still nice and white. The ones at Grüssau were white too. Now I've made my apron dirty. Pappi will scold me. I wonder if the doll can be fixed? I hope the doll can be fixed so Pappi won't be sad any more. There, the church is done. If only Pappi could see it! But

I mustn't tell him that I play here, or he'll be angry. He doesn't want me to be alone. I should play with the other children, he says. But I'd much rather play alone. Giddy-up! Don't you fall, Pappi! That horse is wild.

"I had given her a doll. A very beautiful doll such as you only find in the black market today. She had never owned a doll, although she's seven already. We came as refugees from the East three years ago and we are very poor. It was a big sacrifice for me to buy the doll. We live alone, my daughter and I. We get along well. My wife ran away last year. She was very young and I wasn't able to hold her. Being a priest, you wouldn't know much about these things."

The praying lips paused for a moment to allow certain individuals or opinions to be included in the prayer. When they continued, to the accompaniment of suppressed coughs, tiptoeing steps and rustling clothes, the father's voice also immediately reappeared.

"I'm obliged to leave my daughter by herself for a great many hours during the day. Sometimes a neighbor keeps an eye on her. But I can't often ask her. Then the child is all alone in the room that's been assigned to us or she plays among the ruins. I've found a job as a clerk in the post office. All day long I wonder what the little thing might be doing at that moment. Have you ever pictured a lonely child, Reverend Father? But I meant to tell you about the doll. When I came home last night I saw my daughter in the dim light sitting by the window on her little chair. She had torn the head off the doll and was about to examine the stuffing inside. I flew into such a rage that I struck her. But she did not even cry."

He heard the server's bell. Mechanically his hand made the sign of the cross over the offerings. My God, he thought, here's the Consecration and I am not ready because this man holds me back. He heard him say:

"She tore the doll's head off. That's why I struck her in the face. Who is going to strike me? Then, who is going to strike the one who strikes me? Why can't God for once stop forgiving us? This way it goes on and on. In the end God will be the one who's struck."

In a moment bread and wine will have turned into the body and the blood, he thought, but can I offer sinners forgiveness with that?

Here come the first drops. That's why the tree was rustling so. The rain ghost is coming out of the tree. Quick, the coat for Pappi. The leaves don't stick very well. I must tie a knot with the stems and wrap a blade of grass around. There, now they stick. Now we'll have to drive very fast, like that time we ran from the Russians. That's when Pappi was there all of a sudden. He was still in his uniform. Come on, faster, horsey! We've got to get home. But we went further and further away from home. Too bad Mutti isn't with us any more. I'll take Pappi that piece of mortar with the raincoat. It's got a head like a man. Then he'll be happy again and smile. I wonder if he'll take me out again today and buy me an ice cream. But I mustn't come home wet. I'll stand over there under the cellar door until it stops raining. But only just in front. Inside it's all dark and scary. I wonder what might be inside?

The light figure of the child stood before the dark of the cellar entrance. She waited for the end of the shower which moved its gray-black clouds across the autumn sky. She was clutching the mortar doll and the wooden cart.

The onrushing wave of the Consecration had drawn him into its whirlpool. In a moment he would be cast upon the shore. Here it was. The server's bell rang out three times; the priest bent his knee and elevated the consecrated host with both arms.

"She tore the doll's head off; she was so absorbed in her play she didn't even know what she was doing. And for that I struck her in the face. There is no absolution for that."

"Then why have you come to me? Just to tell me this? You are arrogant, so arrogant that you believe God's mercy could not cover your sin. By the way, you are right; I cannot give you absolution if you don't want God's mercy."

So he went. A man among the ruins, a refugee who believed God would with him perform the miracle of breaking the endless chain of sin and expiation by leaving him in his sin. His eyes were wild with horror—the way the eyes of his child may have been when he hit her. Him, him of all people I should have forced into forgiveness. I should have run after him to the end of the world, pleading with him to accept forgiveness. This once a man's face appeared before me, the priest thought. And I have not recognized it. I have not recognized it. I am not worthy to stand here. And yet, today, I have said Mass for the first time. Mass. Said. His voice was toneless as again he went down on his knees and elevated the chalice. "This is the chalice of my blood, of the new and eternal testament, the mystery of faith," his voice said tonelessly into the silence. But his spirit cried out: "Lord! Why dost Thou strike us?"

Russian Roulette

SIX O'CLOCK. Quitting time. Every day until six because of the five-day week.

He watched the girls pull the covers over the bookkeeping machines and file out into the lounge.

Supervisor in Machine Accounting. For a year now. Ever since I finished office training.

He went into the men's room, washed his hands, studied his face in the mirror.

I look like an office boy. Skinny face. Tip-tilted nose. A couple of inches taller wouldn't hurt either.

Come out all even today?

Klein, that stupid ass. Acting shop-conscious. With his

error quota much higher than mine, too. Hasn't had any offers from other firms either, like I have.

Don't you see I've already closed up, man?

It's all right to ask, isn't it?

Hopeless, that one. Never understands that once you've quit, you've quit.

He slipped into his coat. Went down the big staircase with all the others. Administrative building, chromium plated. Outside the glass walls, the rush-hour traffic flashing by on Grindelallee.

Rush hour. English is a great language. Berlitz. I won't switch to another company. I'll go to America. Or Canada. No draft in Canada.

The big bronze figure down in the lobby.

Quite beautiful, really. "Dynamic Fugue."

Two long, curved arms rising from a shaft, touching at the top.

"Director Steiner Wringing His Hands." All Viscose laughed when I passed that around. It got printed in the company magazine. Steiner "noticed" me on one of his rounds. Silly jokes, that's what they laugh at. Mind you, that thing really is beautiful. Now they laugh at it. Even the ones who never looked at it before. There are times when I hate myself even more than usual.

The evening traffic on Grindelallee went rolling by. Automatic digits of light and matter were being registered. Green: addition. Red: subtraction. Yellow: to straighten out error quotas. The computer for evening communications, feeding on figures. Bookkeeping girls. Supervisor. Signals.

Night and winter overhead.

But what if Canada should be boring? As boring as this place? Then what good would it do me, even if they have no draft over there?

Viscose's seven hundred employees were swallowed up by the underground. He turned off to the left. You were almost alone, if you turned left. The sidewalk, a few pedestrians, then the stream of cars. It was cold. He dug his hands into his coat pockets.

Supposing I played Russian roulette in Canada too, so as to be able to stand it?

She was standing on the edge of the sidewalk, trying to get across. That's how he noticed her. He watched her for a while. Now and then she would timidly step off the curb and quickly pull back again. Two cars almost stopped, the drivers asked her to get in, she didn't respond. Honking. Off again.

He moved closer, stopped three steps away from her. The beams from the headlights sprayed through the pale, loose fur collar around her neck. A student's briefcase. Then he just started across. The car that happened to be next in line skidded around on its rear wheels. It stopped almost at right angles and immediately all the traffic backed up.

Error quota. Supervisor.

The man in the car got out and headed toward him.

You . . . you idiot!

He stopped and waited for him.

I'm sorry! I sometimes get these dizzy spells.

The man gave him a frozen look. He had meant to hit him.

Get yourself a nurse, then! (Pause) Or a seeing-eye dog!

He was shouting. The words "seeing-eye dog" gave him relief. People behind him were honking. He went back to his car.

She understood. He didn't have to make her a sign. She stepped out into the road and together they crossed to the other side, past the cars that were starting up again.

That was a crazy thing to do.

It looks worse than it is. Most of them don't go over forty-five. You can figure on the stopping distance they'll need.

You're a great one for mental arithmetic, aren't you?

No. Just a little guy in machine accounting.

She was on her way to the university. Her face was thin and symmetrical, swept by shadows and lights in the night, its curves and molds carved into the pale wood of the skin. Dark hair, piled up, outlined by a crystal network of light the same as around the fur collar on top of her slim, almost black coat. Wool gloves. Briefcase.

Why did you have to cross over there, of all places? Why not here by the zebra stripes? [1]

I hate zebra stripes.

He nodded. Fair enough. They looked across. The little white pedestrian inside the green traffic light gave his diaphanous signal; on the lines, people were adding up for the evening statistics.

She stopped in front of the university with its gold-lit entrance. On the embankment across the street an S-Bahn train rode into Dammtor Station.

What is it you're studying?

I shouldn't delay her. She only lingers because I took her across the street.

Various things. It is only my second term. I take all kinds of different courses, because I don't know yet what I want to specialize in.

And what is it tonight?

Psychology. It isn't a lecture, though, just a lab. The professor is going to show us a few methods of testing. Rorschach Test, Szondi Test, if you've heard about them.

---

[1] *Zebrastreifen*, slang for street safety zone or pedestrian crossing, indicated by diagonal black and white stripes.

I have, vaguely. As far as I know, they use them to test people's intelligence.

Not just their intelligence. Their whole personality, their character.

I see. (Pause) You have to go in there now? Can't you come and have a cup of coffee with me? Or a grog? It's cold.

Very clever. Now she'll think I want to cash in. For having taken her across the street.

She shook her head. Suddenly she was holding out her hand.

Thanks anyway.

I didn't mean it like that.

I know.

Wool gloves. She turned around and slipped into the university building. The briefcase. The almost black, slim coat.

All over. Oh well, who cares!

One express train and two local S-Bahn trains went by on the embankment as he walked along the street. Between the tracks and the night the sky was cold and yellow. By the square in front of the station he had to wait at the green light to let the ribbon of cars coming from Rothenbaumchaussee go by. Then he saw her again, right by his side.

I've changed my mind. If it's still all right, let's go and have some coffee.

This time they used the safety zone. Over on the other side he headed for Moorweide.

Where are we going?

To the Alster. The café by the Shell building. It's quite passable in there.

Oh yes, I like it.

After the streams of ice under the neon-light moons, Moorweide was an island of dark waters.

Are you from Hamburg?

I was born here.

You like it here or would you rather get away?

Sometimes I'm glad I can still live at home with my parents, other times I can't wait to get away.

My mother lives at Ülzen. But we are from Berlin originally. Ülzen is the end. You know what I mean?

Of course. I can well imagine what Ülzen must be like.

How old are you?

Shit, you don't ask a lady her age.

Nineteen. And you?

Twenty. I've lived in Hamburg four years now. Three years office training and one year in a job. In Viscose, supervisor in Machine Accounting. Eighty-four net.

I must be crazy talking my head off like that. She'll think I'm bragging.

That's a lot. You must be good.

I didn't mean to show off. Can't think why I'm telling you all this.

It's just because I haven't been out with a girl for a year. Since that business with Gafur and Messua. Since Berlin. Since I began playing Russian roulette.

They had stopped under the trees in front of the café. The café sat on floats in the water. From time to time a car went by on Harvestehuder Weg. A street light traced shadows of twigs and branches on their faces and on the bare winter ground.

It's funny. You seem to draw it out of me.

She said nothing. As they crossed the wooden bridge leading to the café they saw the ice on the Alster, white like the kind of white that lies under the night, patches of shadow, that is, blue in the distance. Between the blue of ice and sky the string of lights over on the Uhlenhorst side.

There was practically nobody inside the café. They hung

up their coats. The waiter, a heavy old man, seemed to have water in his legs.

A grog for me. What will you have?

Tea.

She wore a light gray sweater with a V-neck and an ivory-color blouse inside with an open collar. In the light of the room he could see that her hair was dark brown.

I bet I look crummy sitting with a girl like that. Like an office boy.

You like it at the university?

She started up from her thoughts.

Me? Yes, of course.

Must be nice to have that much time for studying.

What you really mean is: to have that much money.

I didn't mean that. (Pause) You're right. I probably did mean it.

It doesn't actually take as much money as you may think. My father earns not even twice what you make.

And on that he lets you take all sorts of courses until you make up your mind what you really want?

He's all right. I am an only child. Maybe he has an Oedipus complex.

What is that?

The waiter came with the glasses. She smiled. He looked away and at the two flat steamboats lying by the bridge outside in the dark, frozen into the ice. The waiter heaved himself off again.

I don't quite know myself. A cliché, meaning the son loves the mother or the father loves the daughter or the whole thing the other way around. It's foolish of me to use words I actually know nothing about yet.

What d'you mean by "love"? The . . . the actual . . .

It's all right in English. Great language.

. . . what they call "to make love" in English?

Yes. But of course, they don't have to do it. That's why it is called a "complex," because they don't actually do it.

So Oedipus complex is just another word for incest?

For the wish for it. Forget it! I shouldn't have talked like that about my father.

He poured the rum into the hot water, then the sugar, and stirred the grog with a short, solid glass stick. Suddenly there was a smell of palm trees and booze, of cinnamon islands and snow ports, velvet blue and rusty red.

Psychology. What do you need that for?

To become a teacher. Or a doctor. For all kinds of careers. Or you take it, just like that. To learn about human nature. Not that studying psychology gives you a better knowledge of people. But it shows you the kind of problems that are possible.

What kind of problems?

Problems between human beings.

Rising slimly from the loose collar of her blouse, her neck moved whenever she spoke. Her skin was light, if slightly darker than the ivory of her blouse.

Is it exciting?

Oh yes, I find most of the courses exciting. Psychology and history and sociology and literature and philosophy. Next term I may take a few science courses.

So you're never bored?

No. Why?

I am. Always.

He felt the revolver in the left back pocket of his trousers, flat, with just the little mound of the cylinder. Instinctively his hand went for it.

She looked at him. Gray eyes in a thin, symmetrical, lively face.

Always?

Sometimes for half an hour I'm not.

When?

When I'm playing Russian roulette.

What is that?

I'll show you later.

But you are good at your job. So, that must interest you.

Oh, hell! You've got to make money so you can afford the few things that'll make you forget the job.

You're just saying that.

Supervisor in Machine Accounting. You know how much brains that takes? No more than it took to handle the petty cash when I was an office boy. That's why I look like one, too.

You don't.

Well, then, what do I look like?

Like someone who takes the reflection of himself for his real image.

And isn't that what it is?

No. It's reversed.

College women. They're full of ideas. I've never had a girl talk to me like that.

Have you ever tried to do something about it?

Yes. I once went to India.

To India?

Yes. But I never got there. Only as far as Berlin.

The waiter stood by the counter, motionless, staring out of the window at the backdrop of the night; the index finger of his right hand was hitched into his sagging vest pocket.

That was over a year ago. Late in the fall of fifty-nine. I was still a trainee then, in my last year. We'd already had the new automatic bookkeeping machines for some time and I had gotten to be quite good at handling them. Monday nights we always used to make out betting slips, Klein and myself, that is. Klein is a fellow I trained with. He's also a supervisor now, but his error quota is too high. They're going to shift him. Have you ever played the pools?

No.

You must. You can win a lot that way. If you're interested I'll show you how to make out a betting slip. Once or twice a week this girl Edith would call for me. I was still going with girls then. Most of the time with Edith, although she always wore a petticoat and acted kind of loud. I can't stand petticoats. You ever wear one?

I've got one.

I can't stand it when people are excited and Edith always acted excited, but then perhaps that's why I got involved with her. She was better than the girls who were just as bored as I was, girls you had to take trouble with to get them a little excited. This Edith was quite fun at times. One day she was waiting for me in a particular state of excitement. She came rushing up to me.

You've won the pool. Three thousand marks. I've just come from your landlady and she told me. An inspector from the betting agency came around this morning. He left a note and said you should come and see them at the office as soon as possible.

Again he was standing in front of Viscose's entrance on Grindelallee on a gray autumn night. Fog. He hissed at her, told her to pull herself together and stop yelling.

You rent a room? From a landlady?

No longer, not since I finished training. I had the company get me an apartment. It's terrific, it really is. Shower bath and everything. A hundred and fifty a month. Viscose advanced me the additional funds toward building expenses.

You're living pretty high. At the age of twenty. What are you going to do when you are forty?

But that's the whole point. That's just what I'm talking about all this time.

They had started smoking. The two boats outside on the Alster were still cutting white shapes into the pale space above the ice.

Go on with your story!

We went downtown like we did every night when we were going to the movies. Dammtorstrasse, Gänsemarkt, Jungfernstieg. That night we made no headway, because she stopped in front of every window to show me the things I'd now be able to buy for myself. Suits, neckties, cameras, furniture. It was fun all right at first. Then it became silly. Just as she was showing me a TV set, I chucked her.

I'm off now.

What did you say?

I said, I'm off.

But you can't just go and leave me like this.

Why can't I? You can go to the movies alone, can't you?

But what have I done?

She had tears in her eyes. It was a mean thing to do. I simply left her and walked away. I just wanted to be alone with the feeling of owning three thousand marks. So on I went alone, first down Jungfernstieg, then off to the right toward Rathausmarkt, then left again up Mönckebergstrasse. Suddenly I saw the neon signs: *Air India*. They were curved and blue.

How did you happen to pick Air India? Aren't there a whole lot of travel agencies on that corner?

I don't know. I once read a book about India when I was living in Ülzen. It seemed to me as though India was the very opposite of Ülzen.

Their glasses were almost empty and the waiter came

shuffling over. He said nothing, just stood there and looked across their heads out of the window.

One more grog! You want another tea?

I should have said "Will you have." Or rather "take." "Will you take another tea?" That would have been polite. I haven't learned a thing. Office worker. While she's an educated girl, college student.

The waiter did not go straight to the counter but stopped at the door to let in a little dog, a mutt that kept jumping up his legs, whimpering with cold.

So I went in. Except for the airline staff there were only Gafur and Messua inside.

Who are Gafur and Messua?

I'm going to tell you.

Gafur wore a brown suit and a white turban. His face was dark. Messua was small and slender with a rather light-colored face. But the darndest thing was that she wore a nose-ring, a little silver nose-ring. In India, she told me later, that is the sign of the married Moslem woman. She had on a raspberry-colored Indian gown. She stood there, waiting. Gafur was reading a letter. They had come to pick up their mail. Wait and read. We can never do that the way they can.

Somewhat flustered, he went over to the desk where they stood, motionless and turban-white and raspberry-red. The airline hostess smiled at him.

They always smile, you know. It makes you puke. When they talk to you they wiggle all over. And they smile. It's as though you'd come into a whorehouse. (Pause) Forgive me.

I want to fly to India.

She smiled.

Always this "want to." "Would like to," is what you should say. Just casually. Always act as though you didn't really want it at all.

When, please?

As soon as possible. Tomorrow.

I was carrying on like a madman. Probably because Gafur and Messua were standing right beside me, making me feel all nervous.

And where to?

Where to? To India!

I mean, where to in India?

Good God, what a blooper! Damn that smile.

Calcutta.

It was the first place I could think of.

We've got a flight at two-forty tomorrow afternoon via Karachi and Bombay. That originates in Berlin, though, with a connection from Fuhlsbüttel, leaving at twelve-fifteen.

How much is the ticket?

Do you wish a round-trip?

Did I wish a round-trip?

He hesitated.

Yes.

That'll be . . . just a moment! . . .

She looked it up on a chart.

. . . two thousand eight hundred and seventy marks.

Which leaves me only a hundred and thirty marks for the stay in India. That's no good.

The palms of his hands were hot. He felt thoroughly humiliated. He watched the devastating smile under the glaring light.

I won in the pool. Three thousand marks. I thought the ticket would be less expensive.

No shadow of sympathy softened the devastation of the smile. In fact, it did not change at all. It stayed exactly the same.

Thank you!

Why don't you fly to Karachi? That'll leave you with almost a thousand marks.

Gafur spoke in English.

I don't speak German well. But I did understand what you were enquiring about. Of course, Karachi is not India; it is Pakistan. Still, you'll find it resembles India quite a lot. We're also flying to Karachi. I must ask the lady how much your ticket is, because we're only going one-way. He looked at the smiling girl, and for the first time it seemed as though she retracted her smile just a little.

That'll be . . .

again she looked at her chart,

. . . two thousand one hundred and twenty marks.

He spoke in English. I never saw anything as crazy as his beard, except in pictures. In pictures of ancient gods, you know. Greek gods, that kind of thing.

Gafur's beard was shiny and black, parted in the middle and twirled into circles on each side with even more curlicues combed in alongside the circles. The beard was a kind of cult, the beard of a god. It was amazing that human words could venture from this beard. Human English words.

My English is quite good, you know. At that time I'd already done two years of Berlitz. And suddenly I no longer felt shy. I think it was due to his beard that I wasn't shy any more. So I managed to thank him and book the flight to Karachi. The smiling girl even gave me the name of a place at the Harbor Hospital where I could get inoculated. She put on a first-rate performance for Gafur. I'm sure his beard had affected her, too. His crazy, solemn beard. I never saw Gafur anything but solemn.

You'd have been fascinated by Gafur, if you'd seen him.

She was smoking again. She did not look at him. A line of concentration had appeared between her gray eyes.

Is she trying to visualize Gafur?

Am I boring you?

No, not a bit. Why do you study English?

Because I'm thinking of going to Canada.

So you aren't quite sure yet?

I'm pretty sure.

Then there is something you are interested in after all. You aren't always bored.

I only want to go to Canada because then I won't have to do military service.

You'll just have to serve in the Canadian army, at your age.

No, there's no draft in Canada.

Why don't you want to be a soldier?

Because I know exactly what it is like when you shoot at a person.

She was looking him straight in the face now. Like a target, she offered him her own acute, sensitive face.

How do you know?

I just do.

The sick waiter brought the second grog. He was breathing heavily as he removed the first glass. Over by the counter his dog was drinking water from a mug. They could hear him slobber.

And there's nothing else about Canada that appeals to you?

No. Why should there be anything special about Canada? I can never think of Canada the way I used to think of India.

Funny. I'd much rather travel to Canada than to India. Her gray eyes. Maybe Canada is different? Gray but lively.

The black Alster outside under the ice. The string of lights from Uhlenhorst. A whole series of soft, gray words came into his mind: wolf's fur, woods, winter sky. For a brief moment her gray eyes looked soft and wolfish. Then again they were clear and straight.

All I saw of Messua that night at the airline office were the purple shadows along her nose. A face as narrow as you find it only in Indian women. You don't believe it until you see it. No, it's only then that you don't believe it. You simply cannot imagine an Indian woman such as Messua. You have to see her to realize that she is unbelievable.

The next morning I ran around in circles. To the betting agency to get the money out, which wasn't at all easy, then to get inoculated, pick up the ticket, invent a story for Viscose why I suddenly had to go off for a few days—they still owed me some vacation—pack a suitcase. But at twelve fifteen I was on the plane to Berlin.

Now I know why you stepped in front of the car just then.

He shrugged. Feigned indifference.

Not for my sake, at any rate. Anyway, I'm just as glad you didn't do it to impress me.

But then, I also did it because I liked you. You looked great standing there, trying to get across.

I've never met a girl like her. She's just great. You can tell her everything.

Gafur gave me a solemn, dignified nod. He made me come over and sit with them. Messua sat between us. Her gown was no longer raspberry-red but bluish-green. She looked bad that morning, I mean, pale with green and purple shadows in a grayish-brown face. Bad but terrific. Gafur looked the same as last night: dark brown, black-bearded and solemn. By the way, he's still young, thirty at the most. Sitting on the plane with Gafur and Messua I no longer felt crummy. Gafur introduced himself. He said: Abdul Gafur. I told him my name. Messua's I found out because he sometimes addressed her by name when he said something to her.

Messua, he admires your dress.

She smiled. She said nothing. All that time the three of us spent together she hardly ever said a word.

It's a sarong, isn't it?

You mean a sari. No. We are Moslems. Only Hindu women wear saris. This is an izar. It is a trousered garment, though you'd hardly notice that. Our women know that the sari is more flattering to the wearer than the izar. So they wear the izar as though it were a sari.

I didn't dare look. Not until later, when we had switched to something else.

You don't look like a Moslem. Only the turban . . .

We call it a pagri. In Karachi you'll learn to distinguish between the various types of pagris. I am a lawyer, that's why I wear a latudar, which is a very tall sort of pagri. You mean we don't look like Arab Moslems?

Yes. You don't look like a fanatic.

Oh, there are a lot of religious fanatics also in our country. But I am a Westerner. I've come to realize that religion must be a private matter. I was a student at Oxford and I represent British companies. By the way, I'm a socialist.

Religion, the West, Oxford, socialism. These were all words from the newspapers. The way he said them, they didn't sound as though they came from the newspapers. As Gafur pronounced them, I felt for a moment that such words might have a meaning. You'd appreciate a man like Gafur!

And you? What is your job?

I am an office trainee.

And you don't like it.

Does that show?

Yes. Besides, you are rushing off to India. Hence you aren't happy where you are. You are trying to escape.

The plane was getting ready to land. I had never been in a plane before and had imagined it to be something wonderful. But it had been boring.

You feel it's wrong to escape?

I don't know yet. I'll have to think about it.

When the plane had come to a halt, Gafur headed for the exit. That moment Messua reached for my hand. She took it, gently but definitely, while we stood side by side and then she brushed her hand along the back of mine. She smiled as she did that. You know how she smiled at me? In a matter-of-fact sort of way. I've thought a lot about that smile later on and I've never been able to find another word for it. It wasn't vulgar, it wasn't brazen, it was tender, rather, and discreet, but it was completely matter-of-fact. It could mean but one thing in the world.

There was a surprise at Tempelhof, because for some reason the plane for Karachi wasn't going to take off until the next morning. Air India did itself proud and put up its passengers at the Hilton Hotel. I was dumbfounded. Never had I dreamt I'd someday stay at that kind of a place in my home town. Come to think of it, I should have enjoyed it, but I couldn't. I was all mixed up since that incident with Messua. I felt ill at ease. You know what? I was scared! And at the Hilton Hotel I felt again like the kind of person I am.

Like the reflection of yourself.

Yes. Crummy. I didn't belong in there. It was plain enough to see. There was a large mirror inside the closet and another one in the bathroom. My suit was the suit of an office boy.

If only I had had the revolver in my pocket then, the way I have now.

Someone ought to tell you how to dress some time. You
don't look as bad as you think. It's just that you wear the
wrong kind of clothes.

Is she the schoolteacher type? No. Not that. She's an
educated girl. Knows more than I do. She tells you things
in a way you can swallow them. The schoolteacher type
wouldn't know how to do that. You can argue with her.

I guess they're the right sort for me. You've only known
me an hour.

Perhaps you're right.

The awkward old waiter had sat down on a chair and
was gazing down at the dog, which had put its muzzle on
one of his shoes.

I had told Gafur that I was from Berlin originally, and
he asked me to show them around the city a bit. I had
visited there last at the age of fifteen with an uncle who
lives in the East Sector and I had no idea how you went
about showing Berlin to somebody. I couldn't show Hamburg to anyone, either. After all, they're just cities with
streets and shops and buildings, nothing else. Of course,
you could show the Alster and the harbor. So I walked up
and down Kurfürstendamm with them until Gafur realized I couldn't do it—show them Berlin, I mean. He went
up to a taxi.

Will you take us to Stalin-Allee?

I really might have thought of that myself. But I was
like a dope that day. I sat with the driver just so as not to
be next to Messua again. I was afraid of Messua. Today it
all seems quite unbelievable. As we were driving I was
able at least to point out Brandenburger Tor and Unter
den Linden to them and the spot where the Schloss used
to be. Gafur had the taxi stop on Stalin-Allee and we got
out and looked at the buildings and the street and the
monuments. Gafur never said a word. He just looked up

and down those buildings. Then we got back into the taxi.

Do you know the cemetery where Bert Brecht is buried?

I knew neither the cemetery nor a man by that name. Would you have known?

Not the cemetery. But I know who Bert Brecht was.

Gafur felt I should have known too. He had seen plays of his in London.

If I knew enough German, I would go and see his plays here, too.

The driver didn't know either, but he asked a Vopo and he knew. That's how we drove to Dorotheenstädtischer Friedhof and visited the grave of a man called Brecht.

If we had a man this great in our country, every child would know about him.

When we were back in the taxi I finally had an idea too.

Seventeen Kantstrasse!

What is there to see?

Another grave.

We drove back into the West Sector. When the car stopped I saw they had torn down the ruins and built a new house on top. Some kind of municipal building.

I don't see any grave.

It is one, though. Under that is where my father is buried.

I guess Gafur felt much more than I did at the time. He sat very quietly for a long while, not looking at the house but with his head bowed.

Where were you then, during the air raid?

Already evacuated, to Ülzen with my mother. It was late afternoon and we stopped our sightseeing. Back at the Hilton I went straight up and stayed in my room. I didn't feel hungry. I'm not often hungry anyway. That time at the Hilton I was scared. I don't know what I was scared of. Of the hotel, perhaps. I was scared being in the room, yet

I knew something dreadful would happen to me if I left it. I was lying on the bed. I had turned on the light overhead. If I could draw I could still make you a sketch of that room even now, the room with my coat flung across a chair, my suitcase that I hadn't even unpacked. The whole thing. I was lying on the bed, smoking. It was after nine when there was a knock at the door. I opened. This time she wore a yellow gown. Lemon-yellow.

The something dreadful came in, dressed in yellow with all its meaning. He did not know that terror and sanctity are yellow. He did not know that the two make up the moment of lust. The light of paradise is yellow. He did not know. Henna and Sindh, it came in, copper and Gondwana, saffron and Ahmadabad, shadow topazes and the Desert of Thar, lemon silk from Gwalior, gold and Baroda, Sindh hands, Gondwana lips, skin from Ahmadabad, Thar shadows, desert shadows, Gwalior silk on Baroda flesh. Golden-yellow and hollowed. It came. In. A houri from paradise. But he never knew. He took her for a whore. To him she was still yellow long after she had turned golden. Later on she was quite different. Come to think of it, later she was a good deal like me. She told me about Karachi.

What do you want in Karachi? It's a boring place. You see the smoke of the ships lying out at sea, waiting to get into the harbor. The rickshaws are nicely painted. Between the sea and the city there are mud flats with white pyramids of salt. That's where the turtles crawl around, scraping holes for their eggs, but in the morning the pariah dogs come and dig them up again. There are factories and slums and a new university. We play cricket. We always play cricket. At this time of year the nights are warm and soft. And still. You won't believe it, but the whole city goes to bed at eight or nine every night. Then it is completely still. Sometimes a bird sits down in front of your window or you may hear the clatter of camel hoofs out on the street.

Why do you go to bed so early?

We are Moslems. In all Moslem cities the nights are still. It's ten o'clock. Where is Gafur now?

He went out. He is sitting somewhere writing a poem. Every night from nine to midnight he writes a poem.

He saw that she was listening without moving. Her thin, symmetrical face was caught in his story and in the twilight of the café as the boats were outside in the ice.

Now she is with Gafur. With his black beard. With his poem. I've managed to mesmerize her with Gafur.

Messua went as suddenly as she had come.

Yellow from my shaded room into the white hallway outside. My sister in boredom.

For a while I remained on my bed, but I couldn't sleep. At eleven, I went downstairs. I didn't have enough courage to go into the Hilton bar. So I sat down in the lobby and waited for Gafur. After a while he came. In his long, black coat, with the white turban on his head, the elaborate beard of a god and the dark brown face, he looked like a maharaja. Everybody turned around for him. He let someone take his coat, then came over to me and invited me into the bar. I ordered a cocktail; he only asked for an orange juice. The bartender seemed to have expected it.

I don't drink.

So you are a . . . a fanatic after all?

I was glad to have a subject.

I live like an orthodox. But I am not a believer. I am a modern and a Westerner. I am strict with myself. That's how I was brought up. Discipline is all that is left of my belief.

I wasn't prepared for his solemnity. It embarrassed me, right there in the bar.

I've been thinking about your escape, whether it is right or wrong. I still don't know. There is still too little I know about you. Last night, when I first saw you, I thought I knew you. I gathered you were naïve the way adventurers are. Since then you have become more and more of a puzzle to me. At your father's grave you were a complete stranger. I wrote a poem about Berlin. In my poem Berlin is a city of cold, gray, empty streets where sons have abandoned the search for their fathers.

Is that why you visit the graves of poets?

Yes.

But I did show you my father's grave, didn't I?

Because the spirit of this poet took you by the hand for a moment. It happened in spite of yourself.

That night at the Hilton bar was the one and only time anyone ever took an interest in me. Maybe my mother does. But she can't express herself. I was amazed that a man who looked like a maharaja and wrote poetry should concern himself with so uninteresting a character as me.

If you came to our country to study meditation, there might perhaps be some point in your escape.

Does meditation mean thinking?

Yes. It is a particular kind of thinking. Actually, it is not just thinking, but a method of doing it. It is an exercise.

How do people do it?

They each find their own way.

Suddenly he no longer seemed to be sitting with me in the bar.

I leave my office around nine o'clock every night. Between nine and midnight I write a poem. From midnight to five in the morning I sleep. Then I get up and take a walk to free myself from the impurities of my body. I return and say a prayer and after that I meditate to drive the impurities from my mind. But my mind wanders, useless things come pouring into it and fill me with new impurity. Later I have breakfast and go to my office.

This Gafur must be a wonderful person!

I've made her crazy with Gafur. Crazy for Gafur. As long as she thinks of him, she is not a student. Gafur turns her into a woman like any other. With me she is just a student, but he transforms her. Gafur undoes her.

But his meditating was all for nothing, since he kept right on getting impure again.

You don't understand. It did make sense all the same.

I see I don't understand anything. For the first time, because she is with Gafur, she is showing me her arrogance. Her educated arrogance.

And what about Messua? Just think of her for a change! It can't be very pleasant for her, living with a man who wants to be pure, just pure.

You stay with a man who is a man no matter what his conditions may be.

She didn't always stay with him, though.

She knew her body belonged to her. Her staying with Gafur had nothing to do with it.

She crushed out her cigarette.

My body also belongs to me. Perhaps my mind does too. Whether or not you stay with a man has got nothing to do with it. I shall never let myself be denied the right to belong to myself.

Well, well. Here's to the man who gets that one. Though maybe this was just another of those college-woman ideas. She might still make quite a good wife.

But didn't you ask him about Messua?

Messua. Then I knew she didn't understand much. Messua, indeed. Messua was still burning inside me like fire. No power on earth could have pried a word about her out of me. It was much more important to tell Gafur that he had been wrong about me.

I can see that meditation is necessary to you. For cleansing, as you say. But it's no use in my case.

How do you mean?

You said your mind fills up, something pours into it.

Useless things. Impurity. Yes.

Anyway, it is something. It's better than nothing. My mind is empty.

He shrank back as though he had touched a poisonous insect. He understood at once. It was sheer politeness that made him disagree after a moment's silence.

I don't believe it.

It is true, though. Why do you suppose I want to go to India? To purify myself? No. I am bored, that's all. I am neither bad nor good. I am empty.

He signaled the waiter for the check. Followed by his little dog, the man came shuddering over and took the money. His vacant eyes added up money, night and death.

Your story is getting more and more depressing.

She seemed to feel chilly. Her beautiful young face had paled, her gray sweater turned to ashes.

It's almost over.

In that case, you need something stronger than meditation. Come along with me, I shall give you something for your emptiness. I sometimes use it against impurity, whenever it becomes too powerful within myself. I am sure it will help your emptiness. When uselessness becomes too powerful you have to fight it with something useless.

They left the bar, he and Gafur. Gafur and Messua had a suite at the Hilton. There was no sound from the bedroom. Was Messua asleep? He watched Gafur open a suitcase and then he saw a revolver in his hand. His first idea was that Gafur had lured him into a trap.

Messua. He knows everything.

But then something much worse happened. Gafur destroyed him in a much more subtle way.

Have you ever held a revolver?

When I was a boy.

This is a six-shooter. You see the cylinder with the six chambers? They are empty. As empty as your mind. Now I am going to put a bullet in one of them. There. Now I pull out the pin that secures the lock.

Silently he watched Gafur, the revolver. What would happen next?

Now I hold the revolver behind my back, you see, like this, I can't see it. And now I spin the cylinder with my other hand. I cannot possibly tell whether there is an empty chamber behind the barrel or the loaded one. Now I raise the revolver so I can't see it and put the muzzle to my head. I always place it inside my ear. That way it can't slip as it might from the temple.

He is mad. Mad, mad, mad.

And then I pull the trigger. There.

The revolver clicked. Nothing. Gafur lowered it from his head and inspected it.

I was lucky. The game is called Russian roulette. Apparently some Russians first started it.

Gafur's face betrayed nothing. Only the very back of his eyes took on an expression of bliss.

You try it! It will help you.

There was no way out. Could he have bolted from the room? It was a trap. It was a trap with an open door. He took the revolver. He flipped the cylinder. He pointed the muzzle to his ear.

The beard. Parted, divided. The parts combed into circles. Black circles of a god. The black shield of the God of Death adorned with a twirl of hair. Rigid. The black ornaments of nothingness. Sindh, Gondwana, Ahmadabad,

Thar, Gwalior, Baroda. The black twirls of India. The Indian eye of the circle.

Click.

And then the unwinding from the eye of the circle, of the barrel, of the twirl. Return from Sindh. The golden light. Paradise. Bliss. Golden, paradisial, Indian bliss. The end of emptiness.

I'll make you a present of the revolver. Also of the bullet. You'll never need another.

He went out and to his room. He took his suitcase, put on his coat, left the hotel and returned home on the inter-zonal train.

What kind of medicine did Gafur give you?

I'm going to show you. Come along, let's go!

Outside they got a last glimpse of the waiter, the old, heavy, sick, doomed waiter in the lit-up cavern of a café. They saw him talking to his dog.

It was cold. He looked around. Someone had laid a plank from the pier to one of the boats.

I can show you over there. It won't take long. No more than a minute.

They walked across the plank and down to the stern of the boat where it was dark, but not too dark. Forward, in the bow, it was too bright with the light from the pier.

Sit down a moment on that bench over there!

She obeyed. He pulled out the revolver. She did not move.

Don't be scared.

She thinks she's been trapped.

It's just a game. They call it Russian roulette.

Floating ice pressed against the sides of the boat. All over the Alster it was white like the kind of white that lies under the night, patches of shadow, that is, blue in the distance.

He explained the game. She listened in silence.

The string of lights over on the Uhlenhorst side.

This is better than sex, you know!

At last she broke her silence.

Lots of things are better than sex.

He noticed the contempt in her voice. For the first time since they had met, she despised him.

I'd like to know what is better than sex. Nothing except this!

The cold. But she did not feel it.

Canada is better than sex.

Wolf's fur, warmth, winter sky. She won't catch me on that this time.

Canada, my eye.

Thinking is better than sex.

He raised the revolver. Put the muzzle into his ear.

It's already lost its effect. Why don't you admit it?

Now she was sneering at him. He became furious. She thought she knew everything. But he lowered the revolver.

How do you know?

That's easy. Once you have done it a few times it's like taking pills.

He stared at her hopelessly, but her face was in the dark. Once again he raised the revolver.

Here, give it to me! Quick!

Suddenly she was on her feet, grabbing him by the wrists.

Why? What do you want it for?

Give it to me! It's a condition. Later you can do with it whatever you like.

Startled, he handed it to her.

Above their heads a train they couldn't see went rumbling across Lombardsbrücke.

She took the revolver. She held it into the diffuse light to get a better look at it. The five chambers were empty. The sixth was behind the barrel.

The rumbling train faded from their perception. Only the ice remained, shadowy blue.

Cautiously she turned the cylinder. The bullet appeared from behind the barrel. She shook it into the palm of her hand. She did it just right. She threw the bullet overboard. It hit the ice and they heard it sing along, skidding away further and further with no echo, until it was silent.

Then she went, across the boat, across the plank, past the café, over the bridge, under the trees.

He saw her under the trees which were tracing shadows all over her.

At last, when he felt the sticky chill of sweat, he realized she had pushed the revolver back into his hand. He was about to raise it, but then remembered he no longer had a bullet.

He hurried over to the trees to catch up with her. Then he stopped. He saw her walk along Harvestehuder Weg until she finally disappeared. He changed his mind and headed for Dammtor Station. The traffic in the city had tapered off.

Sacrifice of a Ram

I HAVE MOVED AROUND a great deal in the past year. In mid-February I went to Switzerland to fetch my daughter, the eleven-year-old. My wife had taken her there the end of January, to an expensive *Kinderheim* at Montana, and after a week we called up to ask her how she was getting along. When she heard my voice she burst into tears. "Why are you crying, beanpole?" I asked her. She grew a lot in her tenth year and for some time I've occasionally called her beanpole. "If you keep on growing like that," I tease her, "you'll get a beanpole husband and beanpole children." She was crying for joy, she sputtered, and because everything was so lovely. It didn't sound very convincing.

"You want to come home?" I asked her. "Shall we come and get you?" "No," she said, "I'm telling you, everything is lovely." She dragged out the word "lovely" in an unnatural way. After she had calmed down a bit she told us that two of the children were down with scarlet fever. My wife and I were alarmed. I asked to be put through to Madame Rollin; she said the two cases of scarlet fever were safely isolated and that Monika was doing splendidly, she was the gayest child in the place and her appetite was excellent. A few days later we called again and again Monika was crying and this time she said she would rather come home. My wife talked to her too; after she had hung up she seemed rather preoccupied and finally suggested that Monika was probably homesick and therefore acting up a bit. I knew she was right but I pretended to sense something more ominous. As I was packing my bag I could feel my wife wondering about my relationship to Monika, but she never said anything. Probably she was also thinking it might be a good idea if I went to see Klaus in Frankfurt some time; I know she disapproves of the way I ignore Klaus, but when every once in a while she asks me to look him up, there is no reproach in her voice. I give her credit for that. She started collecting china a few years ago and since then a change has come over her. Domestic issues no longer seem to interest her very much. This suits me; it makes for a pleasantly cool atmosphere around the house. Incidentally, she is quite wrong if she thinks I have a father-daughter complex about Monika. I simply felt that homesickness in itself was bad enough and you never know what might be going on in a *Kinderheim*. But it was odd that I should have reacted so emotionally. Formerly I would have let the thing take care of itself, not from indifference but because there is an instinct that tells you to leave certain things alone and not interfere. For some time

now I have lost this instinct. Boarding the TEE-train for
Basel at Cologne I felt quite distinctly, for the first time,
that I had lost it. I'm disturbed to find that I now behave
hypersensitively in certain situations; but there's nothing
I can do about it.

From Basel I took the Lausanne express which has a
connection into the Valais. It was already dark when I
arrived at Montana. Up there the air is almost always
extra clear and tingling. I don't much care for the Valais
with its champagne air, its everlasting crystal clearness,
no mists, no intermediate shades. Areas with constantly
high pressure quickly bore me. Was it possible Monika
might be feeling the same way? Besides, at an altitude of
4,500 feet that kind of air makes people emotionally
unstable. I went straight to the *Kinderheim*. Monika did
not dare throw herself into my arms in the presence of
Madame Rollin, the nurses and children, but she stood
beside me trembling with joy. She was suntanned. I satisfied myself that there really was no scarlet-fever epidemic
and that everything else was all right too. Madame Rollin
smiled when I took Monika right back to the hotel with
me. We dined together in the most civilized way. I tried
to sound Monika out, but she had nothing exciting to tell.
The twelve-year-old with whom she had shared a room
was already using perfume, she said. That was all I could
get out of her; nor was there probably more to say; what
would little girls who try out perfume talk about or do
with each other? I did not know and would never find out.
Monika obediently went up to her room and when I
looked in half an hour later she was already asleep, peaceful and relaxed. At the age of eleven she had put on a
couple of first-rate scenes in order to get her way, but now
she was a child again. One of her two little pigtails stood
straight up from her ear. In the morning I would have to

ask the chambermaid to rebraid her hair before we started
off.

I had great sympathy for her hysteria. Too much, perhaps. On the way home, away from the mountain air that
had upset her emotionally, she read through two books
and munched chocolate while I kept wondering why I had
mustered up so much sympathy for her and sacrificed two
days of my time even though I was particularly busy just
then. When the train stopped at Frankfurt I made up my
mind really to look in on Klaus one of these days.

2

After this first attack of nervous sentimentality—an entirely new thing to me—I had a most extraordinary experience in Holland in May. I own shares in a factory at
Alphen—makers of de luxe paper, which is my line of
business—and developments in the Common Market had
made it necessary to negotiate about a merger. Incidentally, the fact that my nervous system obviously is more
irritable than it used to be doesn't hurt me in business; on
the contrary. After the meetings were over, Director de
Vries took me to the train at nearby Leiden. As a rule I
do the Alphen–Cologne stretch by road, but I was without
a car at the time, for I'd already turned in the Mercedes
and hadn't yet received the Lancia. In retrospect even this
switch from one make of car to another seems to me a
result of the recent disconcerting developments in my
emotional life. I used to swear by a car's stability and
rugged performance, nothing else; yet I remember distinctly how, from the moment I saw it, the large bird-
smooth Lancia Flaminia sedan became an obsession with
me. Suddenly that heavy, solid fellow in my garage would

no longer do. I was crazy for a car that made me want to caress it whenever I saw it.

We were early arriving at Leiden—it was only three o'clock and my train was not leaving until shortly after four—and de Vries took me around the town, which is not very big and as Dutch as can be. It happened as we were walking along Rapenburgwal. Rapenburgwal is a *"gracht* street,"* which means that there is a green canal lined with linden trees in the middle and roadways on both sides just wide enough to let a car go through. From time to time a bridge reaches across the canal, on which float black barges. The houses on both sides of Rapenburgwal are large, old and beautifully kept; some of them are palaces dating back to Holland's golden century. Now, these houses—this is what I mean when I say: it happened—these houses were whispering. I no longer heard what de Vries was saying. With the collar of my raincoat turned up I crept past the whispering houses, hunched over, distracted. Although I strained my ears, I could not understand a word of their whispers; but there was not the slightest question that they were softly talking to each other. I suffered a shock of anxiety, immediately suspecting, of course, that this was the beginning of a mental disorder, the first symptom of a psychosis. After all, people become insane the same way they get cancer or leukemia. As we reached the end of Rapenburgwal, de Vries asked me if I was not feeling well, I looked so pale all of a sudden. I told him I was all right, although my back was cold with perspiration.

I managed to say goodbye to him at the ticket office inside the station and proceeded to the platform. But instead of getting aboard I headed back to the exit after the train had left. Making sure that de Vries' car had disappeared from the square outside, I hurried back to the old city. As I turned into Rapenburgwal I found I had not been mistaken. The houses were still whispering. This time I made my way slowly and quite calmly along the *gracht*. Despite my fear, I made myself stop now and then to look at the houses. They had green and black and dark red doors with highly polished brass knockers and their large white-framed windows were set in walls of rusty brick. They had a strange look. The night before, at the hotel at Alphen, I had had a dream I could no longer remember except that in it I had been naked and the skin all over my body had been dark green. In that dream I had felt as strange to myself as these houses were strange. Incidentally, they were no longer whispering now, but had started to sing. They sang softly, huskily, on one note. Their song was compact, monotonous, menacing. Above them the sky was a pale, quiet blue, a typically Dutch sky in May. From time to time cars passed me. I was afraid. No doubt, I had fallen victim to a hallucination.

Seeing trees at the end of an alley, I turned into it and came to a public park. It had gotten late. I sat down on a bench and began to smoke, little Dutch cigars. They soothe me. I smoke either black cigarettes, Gauloises, or, especially when I want to relax, those small, light brown Sumatra cigars. While I was smoking I gradually began to realize what it was I wanted. I wanted to stay in Leiden. I was seized by a very definite and urgent desire to get lost to the world. I would have to begin by taking a room at a hotel; after that I would try to rent an apartment in one of the houses on Rapenburgwal, for it was absolutely essential to get behind the secret of their singing, to live with their whispers. After a time the attack subsided. I felt it would be difficult to disappear without a trace. Ordinary people might get away with it, perhaps, but I am a leading industrialist in my line, fairly well off and endowed with what you might call tradition, family, background. At last I became again conscious of my surroundings. I was sitting in a very beautiful garden with old trees, flowering shrubs and beds of softly colored tulips. Young people with brief-cases were walking about, and as I was leaving I realized that this was the garden of the University of Leiden. The houses on Rapenburgwal had ceased to whisper and sing as in the falling dusk I walked to the station.

3

Fortunately, since then I have been spared such alarm-ing hallucinations. However, this one was enough to make me consult Professor Thiele at Frankfurt immediately after my return. Thiele has been my doctor for years; he is an internist of international fame, but it is not on account of his reputation that I go to him. I have little confidence in doctors; the older I get, the less trust I put in people anyway. But in Thiele's case I discovered that he gives himself away by a change of pitch in his voice when-ever he thinks he has found something serious. That is a great advantage; most doctors are expert liars. Thiele examined me and seemed very pleased. "You've gotten slimmer, Herr Jonen," he said, nodding approval. For some years I had put on weight and I looked back to that time with disgust. Then, two years ago, almost from one day to the next, I began to rearrange my life; without too much effort I kept to a rather elaborately worked-out diet and started playing tennis, tentatively at first but then with real vigor. Since then I have lost almost all my paunch, though I am still rather the heavy type, certainly not a lightweight. Thiele was not too pleased with the electro-cardiogram, but he said there was no reason to worry as long as I did not have any complaints. It sounded sincere. He warned me to be careful about smoking. I told him my experience at Leiden. He listened very attentively, then for a time tapped the top of his desk with his fingers. "The menopause," he said finally, "the male menopause. That's when a thing like this may occasionally occur. A bit early in your case, Herr Jonen. You'll only be fifty two years from now, right?" I carefully listened to his tone of voice but could detect nothing special. "How about inter-course?" he asked. "Everything all right?" He probably did not expect an answer to this one, for he immediately added: "You could always have yourself analyzed. Might not be such a bad idea, perhaps, in your case." This time there was something wary in his voice, something insidious and watchful. Thiele is a tiger of a doctor after all; he lies in wait and then pounces on his patient just at the right moment. "Zurich is the only place for that," he ordered, handing me the address of a psychoanalyst there. "Will cost you a small fortune," he said, "but it's worth it."

Once I was downstairs on the sidewalk by the Taunus mall I felt greatly relieved. The usual symptoms of wear and tear aside, I was by and large healthy. My recent emo-tional extravagances did not stem from some organic illness. Consultations in Zurich to have them diagnosed and removed were out of the question; I felt old enough to be able to cope with my little neurosis, or whatever it was.

At that moment my new sensitivity played me another trick. I remembered Klaus and decided to look him up. I often go to Frankfurt and each time I remember that Klaus lives there, but so far I had always refused to see him again regardless of my wife's pleas; she visits him from time to time and slips him some money. Supposedly he is there to study, but knowing him as I do I am sure he just attends lectures off and on and lives by odd jobs and the shady favors of strange friends. He does things that are crooked. He is enormously gifted; what other people take two hours over, he can do in ten minutes and do well; he also does crooked things. He does them sort of on the side. Actually, he would like to do things that are big and straight and good. But he has no perseverance. Come to think of it, he is always sad, full of aimless, irrepressible sadness; but he is sad without being sentimental and so he can be very gay and witty and entertaining. I'm sure he is a wild success at parties. When he had had enough of us, when there was nothing more for him to learn at home, he left, six months before he was to have finished school. At first he was only gone for a week and then came back, quite apologetic even, but a month later he left for good. The second time I no longer looked for him, and I asked my wife not to look for him either. He bummed around the south all summer and then we heard through friends that he had settled down in Frankfurt. Finally he even sent us word. He seemed to be having quite a rough time.

As I was sitting in the taxi I was surprised to find I even knew his address by heart. And not only did I remember his address by heart but Klaus himself, just the way he is. I felt irritable and had misgivings. Leipziger Strasse turned out to be noisy, shabby lower-middle-class, ringing with streetcars. I knew through my wife that he lived in the basement of Number 78. The basement was set up as a business office, but it was dusty and looked deserted. I spotted Klaus behind a partition at the far end. Though it was going on noon, he was still in bed, but in no time at all was up and dressed. He gave no sign of surprise when he saw me but seemed genuinely pleased. "Oh, it's you, Father," he said. We walked along Leipziger Strasse and back for a few minutes, talking about his studies. I professed to take them seriously. Klaus is tall and lean and black-haired; he looks smart even in the shabbiest togs.

I have no idea where he gets his elegant looks; certainly not
from me. I pumped him about girls, but apparently there
wasn't any particular one on his mind. While I was walking up and down with him I realized there was absolutely
nothing one could do to help him; but at the same time I
had the distinct feeling of having failed with this boy,
irrevocably failed. It was a horrid feeling. I gave him two
one-hundred-mark bills and he took them in just the right
spirit: without a trace of either servility or arrogance, just
simply and quietly pleased. He lit a cigarette; I watched
him and noticed that his hands were shaking. Standing in
the street, we talked for a bit about various things, and all
the time his hands were shaking. It really upset me;
formerly, before I had these attacks of irritability, the sight
of Klaus's shaking hands would not have upset me in this
way at all. I suppose I must have been in some kind of a
daze, for it never occurred to me to ask him to lunch with
me. Instead I fled. I said goodbye hastily, got on a street-
car and went back downtown.

4

Back home in Cologne I told my wife about my visit
with Klaus. She listened, the way she does, with no visible
emotion. Since she started collecting porcelain she has
become cool. Cool and smooth. It was after dinner and we
were sitting in the big living room of our house at Thielen-
bruch. I had the house built six years ago by a modern
architect and my wife decorated it with great taste, not
with the usual mixture of Knoll International and baroque
you find everywhere nowadays, but with some old Rhenish
pieces, wooden chests from the Eifel and cabinets from
around Jülich, inheritances from our two families. In a
modern house those things don't seem heavy, just serene

and luxurious. My wife's father owned a brickyard at Rheine, so she, too, comes from an old family of industrialists, from an industry which, like paper, is more a trade than an industry. She is small, skinny and always immaculately dressed. In the last few years her hair has begun to get gray, so she touches it up discreetly to a darkish red. She is still very pleasant to look at, aside from the fact that she has almost no chin. I never used to notice that so much; now it bothers me more and more. Also she wears too much jewelry; it makes her glitter and jingle, which gets on my nerves.

"Nice of you to have found your way to Klaus at last," she said when I had finished my story. I had a cutting reply on the tip of my tongue, but at that moment Monika came in to say good night, already in her pajamas. She snuggled up to me and started into the elaborate good-night ceremony she always puts on so she can stay up a little longer. Our living room has a huge window, and while Monika was going on about her school I looked out at the red neon sign of the big Wulle breweries at Dellbruck. When I built our house it was still completely surrounded by woods. Two years ago the city had the wooded area to the southeast cut down. Since then we look out every night from our picture window at the red neon signs. It makes you laugh to think that you go and build a house for a quarter of a million D-marks, to see not the stars at night but just the red, blazing word *Wulle*.

"Monika, you really must go to bed now," my wife said, and Monika obligingly took her leave without making a distinction between us in the tenderness of her kisses. She is a clever child.

When she had gone I said to my wife: "You never told me that Klaus's hands were shaking. In fact, you never told me at all how things really are with him."

"Are his hands shaking?" she asked, somewhat surprised. "I never noticed."

For several years now I have had affairs with other women, ladies from among our friends. Such episodes invariably get started at parties we go to or ones we have at our house, the way people do these days. They always have a great appeal at first; a strange woman—there's something mysterious about that. It has a certain allure to begin with, even though in our social set there usually isn't too much risk involved. I don't know whether this live-and-let-live of ours is a sign of being civilized or of a particularly perverted kind of barbarism. By the way, I could have given Professor Thiele a perfectly clear and reassuring answer to his question. In the end I am usually glad when such affairs are over; the longest one lasted six months and I still have sentimental memories of it. I have no idea whether my wife notices these things; she certainly doesn't show it. Her hobby seems to occupy her fully. Someone once explained to me that a collector's passion easily turns into something morbid.

"Oh well, you know," I heard my wife say with a laugh, "Klaus is a wonderful actor. He has a great knack for rousing pity, if he wants to."

I could not bring myself to look at her, I hated her so at that moment. Instead, I looked at the glass case which holds her porcelain collection. It is to the left of our big picture window and stands clear from the wall so one can walk around it and look at the pieces from all sides. My wife collects mainly Chelsea, but she also has a few good pieces of Old Berlin. I can't really see anything in this stuff, at best I find it pleasant, but it hasn't made my wife pleasant, just cool and smooth. Once I attempted to give her mania a new turn by bidding for her at an auction at Boerner's for a Chinese piece that had caught my eye at first glance—a reclining ram, very old, with a jade-colored glaze, powerful, tremendously simple, with no decoration at all. She had admired it very much. "But, you know," she had said, "that is not porcelain, of course, but pottery." Nevertheless, she had tolerated the ram in her collection or perhaps simply had not dared remove it for fear of hurting my feelings. It had been sitting there among the dainty European pieces ever since—wrapped up in itself, menacing and strange.

Suddenly I got up and crossed over to the glass case. The little key was in the lock; I opened the door and took the ram out.

"What are you doing over there?" I heard my wife say in a low, tense voice.

"I am an actor too," I said. "Like Klaus," I said, "maybe not quite as wonderful."

I still wasn't looking at her, but I knew she had gotten up and was watching me, standing rigidly, her back to the window with the word *Wulle* shining in red behind her.

With all my force, I smashed the ram down on the floor. Our living-room floor is laid with gray stone tiles and there was no rug where I stood. The ram disintegrated into a thousand pieces. When you drop a piece of pottery it doesn't break; it actually crumbles. The ram was not broken; it had dissolved into a pile of clay crumbs; suddenly—how shall I say?—suddenly it wasn't there any more. It had disappeared as if by magic.

Now I looked at my wife. She was still standing there rigidly, her left hand clenched and pressed against her mouth. This way I could no longer see that she has no chin at all. She stood for another moment and then, very quickly, went out. Her jewelry was jingling.

For a time I looked at the spot where she had stood and then again at the clay crumbs at my feet, and suddenly I had to laugh. I had done a thing the cartoonists make fun of: I had thrown dishes. That my dishes had been a two-thousand-year-old Chinese funerary piece, something which has been written up in standard works on archaeology, could not take away from the fact that I had behaved like a figure in a cartoon.

I went out into the kitchen, took a brush and dustpan, and swept up the crumbs. I then emptied a cigar box and put the remains of the ram inside, went into my study—which is also where I sleep—and hid the box behind some books. I took a luminal. Not only have I gotten to be hypersensitive, I thought, not only am I the proud possessor of a neat little neurosis that borders on a mental disorder, I am even beginning to have regular hysterics. I had a few depressing moments before the luminal took effect.

Diana with Flute Player

COUNTESS DIANA was about six foot two. That is a lot for a woman. When she wandered down the Blauort beach, with the two large dogs romping by her side, she cut a tall, scrawny silhouette into the horizon for the fishermen out on the edge of Korbbaken Sand. In all the sixty-two summers she spent at Blauort, she never wore anything but twill trousers stuffed into high rubber boots and a shabby old leather jacket. Except on very hot days. Then she would lie stark naked in some sandy hollow, lolling in the sun and forgetting that no one had ever told her that she wasn't really scrawny or too tall for a woman. Only her father had sometimes caressed her and said: "You certainly are a beanpole, child, but you have a peculiar beauty all your own." Indeed, her silky, transparent skin enveloped the thin body like sleek plumage, and sometimes when she walked she reminded one of a tall, beautiful bird, a watchful heron perhaps. But nobody seemed to notice that, and if anyone ever had, he had not mentioned it. People don't like to pay compliments to a woman who is ugly at first glance. They fear that flattery might enhance rather than soften her shortcomings. The ugly, beautiful Countess Diana had come to realize this early in life and had retired to Blauort. Whether or not that was a good thing is hard to say.

Up there, of course, no one had a chance to notice what Diana's father had called her "own peculiar beauty." For during the sixty-two summers of her remaining years—she reached almost ninety, by the way—she only saw the farmer from Nordstrand who took care of shearing her sheep each year; sometimes a few fishermen who had failed to reach the Hever stream before low tide and used the enforced leisure to call on the countess and sample her famous Dutch gin; or an archaeologist now and then who thought he might still find some odd potsherd on the tidal flats of Rungholt. Thus, little chance for courtship; but that was how the countess herself had decided it. She was a great lady with a dislike for chance and a weakness for decision. And so all the admiration she now evoked lay in the small area between the mouth and eyes of some crab fisherman who sighted her tall, scrawny silhouette as he drifted along the edge of Korbbaken Sand. His mouth never puckered into a mocking grin, yet the corners of his eyes filled with an affectionate smile: that was her victory. But of this neither she nor the fisherman was aware.

Between the two wars the countess spent the winter months of each year in Rome. She hated her Holstein relatives and could not bear sitting through a winter among furniture that offended her taste, especially when she thought of the architectural nobility of the manor houses that held it. Since the Retzlaffs had begun going to Bayreuth each year, they had become interested in Norse mythology and had redecorated their two houses on the marshes with Lenbach-style furniture which they bought from a cabinetmaker at Munich. Diana rescued the best pieces—a few Frisian chests and the quiet Danish Bieder-meier—for Blauort. She never again entered her cousin Detlev von Retzlaff's house when she found after the First World War how the breath of vulgar political conspiracy had begun to invade it; it seeped from the carved "Wotanic paneling"—as she called the Munich monstros-ities—into rooms once governed by the homespun grace of music by Telemann and Buxtehude. "It's a disgrace," she told Detlev. "You are ruining the whole countryside with that gang of yours. Don't you know that we set the style for the farmers all along the coast?" Detlev had tried to convert her, but without success. Through all his talk she had heard the slogans of the gang. It was a disgrace! A Retzlaff talking like someone trying to peddle rotten merchandise. "It's either me or that brown-shirt gang!" she had announced in the end. But Detlev had already been committed too far. He was a Frondist, as was the countess too by the way; but there is a great difference whether you plot to the sounds of "Rheingold" or with your ears open to the honking of the wild geese over Blauort.

Late in the fall of 1934 she met in Rome a man who finally became something like a devoted admirer, or in any case a friend.

That was Father Spontini, who lived in the little Olivetan monastery by the Porta San Paolo, *"fuori le mura*," as he liked to point out jokingly. "I, too, live outside the walls, Contessa Diana," he would say with a smile, "just as you do on your island in the far north." Diana had met him one night at the Oriolos. She liked to go to the Oriolos because she knew the old prince never invited Fascists. As for the rest, she avoided social life, and staying in a quiet English pension near the Spanish Steps, she was almost as isolated in Rome as she was at Blauort. She did, however, visit the small, noisy movie theaters, thick with cigarette smoke, and saw all the films which then no longer could be seen in Germany: Bergner as Catherine the Great or the latest Chaplin movies. Spontini had been described to her as a top authority in Etruscan research. She found him charming. He was small and slight, yet just as dignified as she herself, and since she could not bend down to him, nor did he want to talk up to her, they compromised by standing side by side and addressing their words as if to an imaginary third person, although no one ever joined them during the half hour they chatted in this position. When they parted, the padre was bold enough to tell her that he had never seen anything less Etruscan than the Contessa. He said that, pointing to a clay tablet from Cerveteri, painted with figures the archaic crudeness of which could hardly be outdone. The Oriolos had had the tablet set into the wall of a niche. "A dead woman being abducted by a demon, an archer in the foreground," Spontini explained and was gone. Diana inspected the figures closely and found that she had been paid a compliment.

She met the padre quite by chance on one of the following days when she was about to enter the Protestant cemetery near the Pyramid of Cestius. "Where do the flowers go?" he asked her bluntly, pointing to the roses she carried. "To Shelley's grave," she replied. "You like his poems?"

He did not wait for an answer but began in fluent if somewhat unusual English to recite the first two lines of "The Cloud." The very northern poem, with its rich, flowing water colors, sounded strange among the gravestones under the cypress trees; strange coming from the mouth of the frail monk, whose face stood sharply outlined in black above the white cowl of the Olivetans. "Many people have made good poems," the countess said, trying to shake off the mood. "I bring him flowers because he was drowned in the sea." "Of course, he had sailed out too far," she added somewhat reprovingly. And after a pause: "Have you ever sailed too far out to sea, Father?" Spontini shook his head. He glanced at her imperceptibly from the side as she stalked along among the graves, overly tall and much like a long-legged, watchful shore bird. No doubt, he thought, she takes the offering to the dead Englishman because she knows so well what it is like to lose sight of land, drifting on the perilous surge of the current, face turned up to the clouds until they descend in a Cimmerian death. "A dead woman being abducted by a demon," he thought, suddenly recalling the tablet that had served him for a joke, a joke he held her with. In the north where she lives, he thought, there won't be an archer to bring down the demon. But there he underestimated the countess, who was her own archer, a Diana of the northern hunting grounds who never shot duck other than in flight and only from her three-barrel shotgun. She changed the subject they had barely touched upon. "And you? What are you doing here in the Protestants' graveyard?" she asked him. "I live over there," he replied, pointing to the low roof of his monastery which showed behind the wall. "I often go walking," he said, "and I like to live close to the apostates."

"You like your heretics dead?" He laughed. "Dead

heretics can be far more dangerous than live ones," he replied. "Besides, Contessa, don't you know that there are no dead?"

The proof came to Diana only years later, on a summer night at Blauort. During the winters before the war she went for many walks with Spontini. At her request he showed her the most important Etruscan finds in the Vatican and in the Torlonia Museum, and sometimes she rented a car and drove with him to Tarquinia, Orvieto, Chiusi or other centers of this early culture. Once she tried to make him go to a Chaplin movie with her, but he declined. However, he made her describe the films she saw in great detail. Throughout their acquaintance the padre never once made an attempt to convert her. He knew that the countess was not a Catholic, yet he also knew that she never attended a Protestant service. Had she been baptized at all? Once when they were visiting the Tomba del Triclino, one of the dark, mysterious burial sites of Tarquinia, he asked her abruptly: "Is Count Detlev von Retzlaff your brother?"

"No, he is my cousin," Diana answered with surprise. "Why do you ask?"

"No particular reason," the padre replied. "I hear he has founded a new religion, a German cult."

"Yes," said the countess, "he told me. He came to see me on the island for that very purpose last summer."

She smiled to herself over the phrase *"credere al tedesco"* which Spontini had used. "And?" the padre inquired. "Was he successful?"

"I told him he had only two hours before high tide and that he had better hurry if he wanted to get back with the horses in time. You see, at low tide my island can be reached by carriage from Nordstrand," she added in explanation. And they went on to discuss the natural phenomena of tidal flats, which the padre never tired hearing about.

Back at Blauort, memories of the Etruscan tombs caught her now and then in her sleep. In her dreams the figures of the Tomba del Triclino became alive. She particularly recalled a flute player who suddenly leaped from the austerity of an Attic vase to perform a wild dance. Flute at lips, he pranced around her, a little man with a white chiton flapping around his red body, mocking her with his eyes. Sometimes his features would change into those of Charlie Chaplin or Father Spontini. Then Chaplin's little mustache gleamed phosphorescently in his dark face—like the negative of his familiar mask—and the white Olivetan cowl shrank into a short chiton. "You are much too tall for a woman," she heard the padre say. "You may as well believe the German way," Chaplin sneered. She herself could not utter a word; her mouth was frozen, and when she looked down she found to her horror that she had turned into the center column of the Tomba, into a winged angel of death carved from stone, with legs ending in serpents. Far below her the flute player, the monk and the comedian were dancing in a circle around Typhon.

One night in June, well along in the war, she woke from one of these dreams. Lighting the candle by her bed, she remained for a few minutes rigid under her covers as though in death. She was already eighty at that time. Without changing her position she gazed at the heavy old chest underneath the window, which she had chosen as her coffin. On it the workman had carved these words in old Low German: "The Frisians shall be free," a phrase from Frisian common law. "As long as the winds shall blow from the clouds and the world shall stand," the countess added under her breath. In her heart she always hoped that some day a great flood would wash her and Blauort away. But if that wish did not come true, the old chest would do best. Outside, the silent walls of night echoed the faraway, high-pitched drone of British air squadrons; they carried it into the room and to the ears of the countess.

Diana got up and dressed. When she had pulled the door shut and stood outside, the noise of the engines sounded stronger rising and ebbing in waves, a raucous chorus blared into the air. The planes were flying east; already the first squadrons must have passed the coast line. Diana could see the flashes from the anti-aircraft batteries near Husum. In almost glaring moonlight the receding tide revealed wastes of salt flats and sands, shimmering silver or fading like a soft haze into the dark. At the northern tip of the island the curve of the mussel bank cut like a white chalk mark into the luminous blue. Diana noticed a stir among the sheep huddling closely on the grassland to the south and heard scattered cries from the large glaucous gulls which had their nests on the south shore and were usually asleep at this hour. When the noise from the planes had faded, silence set in again. The old woman leaned against the wall of the house and gazed at the gleaming white umbels of the elderberries she had planted with such care. Only then did the distant sounds of a flute reach her ear. She listened. There could be no mistake—someone was playing a flute far out on the salt flats. The sounds, scattered by no breeze in that still night, came from somewhere in the north, from around the Rungholt flats. Within moments the countess had mastered a sudden impulse of fear. She went back into the house and got her walking stick, but she did not take the dogs or her shotgun, reckoning that a person who played a flute far out in the watery wilderness at this hour could hardly be up to any mischief. She left the island by the north shore and for a while wandered across the firm, fluted sands, following the sounds. Now and then the music would cease. Then she stopped and waited until it began again. After a time she was able to discern the tune that was being tried over and over again, a few simple bars attempting to produce "The Last Rose of Summer." Looking back, Diana could no longer see even a glint of Blauort. On her right to the north she heard the roar of the Hever, which gradually was filling up again with water. Then, out of the dark and in the leaden light of the moon appeared the outline of the old water-well left from the great flood of 1362; sitting on its rim, his back turned toward her, the figure of a man.

The man heard the crunch of a shell under her footstep. Turning around, he lowered the instrument and stood up. "Oh, hello," he said as though he had expected Diana. "Good evening, madam!" and, also in English, he added: "At last, a human being." He wore a long, sleeveless leather vest over a cloth jacket. There really wasn't much more to him than a pale, young face under blond hair, a face which gradually filled with surprise as it reflected the amazement of the countess.

"Who are you?" she finally managed to say.

"Captain Miller of the Royal Air Force," the young man replied.

"And what are you doing sitting out here?" the countess snapped. "Don't you know the tide is due in an hour?"

"Tide?" he asked in surprise. "But am I not on the coast?"

"Nonsense," she said. "You are in the middle of the tidal flats and if you stay here tooting away on that flute of yours you're going to drown."

"It isn't my flute," the captain said. "I found the thing, walking across the sand just now. Here, have a look." He handed her the instrument. It wasn't really a flute but a little ocarina of mud-colored clay. Diana was stunned. It was an ancient object, originally from Rungholt no doubt, from the Edomsharde that had been washed away six centuries ago; she had seen one instrument much like it in the museum of Husum. This one was chipped a bit, but it still played. She gazed at the young Englishman. A strange fellow, this, obviously shipwrecked, making a rare find and immediately putting it to use by calling for help. But then, perhaps he wasn't so strange, but simply in the service of the one to whom Diana had brought roses all these years, the caprice of a poet whose songs had driven him out to sea and who now returned from the sea as a song. As they walked toward Blauort, young Captain Miller told her that his reconnaissance plane had been forced down somewhere on the North Sea. His copilot had been killed, he said. There had been just enough time to launch the rubber raft before the plane sank. Then he had drifted three days and two nights. On this, his third night, a western current had thrown him onto the sandbank of the Hever. Thinking he had reached the coast, he had left the boat and walked east. The old water-well seemed to confirm his belief that he would soon come upon human habitation. "And why didn't you walk on?" the countess asked. "I heard you playing for almost two hours." "I had only just found the thing," he said, "and it fascinated me. Besides—what am I missing? They'll get me behind barbed wire soon enough."

The incoming tide was already wetting their shoes as they reached the island. By now the moon was low on the horizon, but there was still enough light for the Englishman to take in the house and the mussel bank, the elderberry bush and the sheep on the grassland to the south. "No other people here except you?" he asked in surprise. At the house she gave him blankets and assigned him the bench in the front hall to sleep. Before she went off to her room she told him: "You may stay here. As long as you remain on the tidal flats you are free. That is Frisian law. Besides," she added with just a trace of feminine guile, "you can do no more harm here than if you were sitting in a camp over on the mainland." She did not wait for an answer, just said, "Think it over!" and left him.

They talked little to each other in the weeks that followed. In the daytime, Diana roamed the island or the salt flats, sometimes shooting a duck or a brant or taking one of her endless sunbaths, while the captain sat inside the house to avoid being seen from one of the fishing boats, rare though they now had become. He read all the English books in the library and only went out at dusk or in the night. He started a collection of all the different shells he found, and now and then returned with a net full of mussels. But most of the time his walks would end on the beach, where he lay for hours playing the ocarina from Rungholt. The gentle tune of "The Last Rose" often accompanied Diana to sleep. One night in a dream she was back again by the old well. Again the moonlight gleamed and again a man played the flute as he sat on the rim. Like young Miller he wore a long leather tunic, but when he turned and got up Diana saw instead of the aviator a bearded man of uncertain age. "So you have come at last," he said to her in ancient Frisian. "It's your turn now." He was about to hand her the ocarina. Diana shrank back. "Go on, take it!" he urged. "I have played it ever since the great deluge. 'You will be relieved when the next flood comes,' the death-bird told me at that time. How long ago that is now!" he added, as though to himself. "Ever since, I have wandered about in these wild waters that overtook us when we made the priests give the sacrament to a sick sow." And he actually began to cry. Diana

was appalled. "But where is that great flood you are talking about?" she asked him. "The sea is calm. Why should
I relieve you?"

"You must," the man said slyly. "Listen up there in the
sky."

And indeed the sky again was filled with the metallic
roar of planes. "This time the great flood will come from
the sky!" At these words Diana woke up and listened out
into the night. The bomber squadrons were coming over
the island; their wild song was rushing through the world.
This time the old woman did not light a candle. She
thought of the poem by Shelley that begins: "When the
lamp is shattered the light in the dust lies dead." Then she
remembered how Father Spontini had claimed that there
were no dead. She smiled, half in sleep. Was there anything the padre did not know? There was one flaw in his
knowledge, though: it came to him from others. Never had
he himself seen the black rites of Tarquinia or heard the
cry of the death-birds over the northern sea or Chaplin's
silent laughter—to him in his cell the reports of these
things were enough. And so, imbedded in his knowledge
sat the sharp hook of steel that tore him away from life.
With such thoughts Diana now fell into a dreamless sleep.

Next morning she found a sheet of paper on the table
in the front hall. "Thanks, grand old lady!" it said. "But
staying here would mean escape." He would use the night
and low tide to cross over to Nordstrand and turn himself
in at the first coast-guard station. The ocarina was lying
by the letter.

Diana understood his motives. Nevertheless, she was
sorry that he had failed to grasp that according to the old
custom the wilderness is still sacred soil. Mourning for her
young companion, she stood staring from the window out
to sea. Only after desolate minutes did she feel that she

was free—though free at the high cost of loneliness. The clock in the hall continued ticking. Her old hand folded mournfully around the ocarina. She knew it was still full of songs.

A Lover of Half-Light

HIS MOTHER took a long time getting ready today, which was odd, considering that she was usually such a quick one. At seventy-three she was still the determined, sprightly little lady she had been all her life. Her lingering should have struck Lothar Witte, but it did not strike him at all; not until later that afternoon, shortly before the accident at Barrentin, was he to learn why his mother had dawdled around the house that morning until she finally appeared, walking down the garden path of the villa at Frohnau toward the Opel where Lothar sat waiting, half impatient, half dozing, since he had put in her two suitcases fifteen minutes earlier. He sat and stared out at the suburban street with the green foliage overhead, at the dull house with its light gray paint where he had lived until the end of the war and where his mother had stayed on—she now rented the main part to other people—and he realized that he was staring at the years with Melanie without any particular feeling. For years now, whenever he came to Berlin, he had been able to go out to his mother's and walk about the house without having the thought of Melanie drive him into wild fits of temper, the way it had at first following that October morning in '47 when she had so completely and irrevocably disappeared. Fourteen years later that was all over, must be over, if Lothar could sit and wait here drowsily instead of starting the engine instantly and driving off. But he did not even think of this, thought only fleetingly of Melanie at all, just as he had long ago stopped mentioning her name to her husband, Richard Brahm. One day, as if by mutual agreement, they had put an end to their Melanie cult, had given up the attempt to make a fetish of her memory. Her shadow—a shadow so transparent and luminous as to be cast only by fragile, brown-skinned Melanie who loved to dress in thin fabrics of pure, light, almost faded colors—had appeared in their talk only when they had to make a decision concerning the children. Then Brahm had come from Hanover to Cologne for anxious consultations with Lothar; the children had been difficult and costly. The two men had tried one school after another but it had never worked. The children had been a headache. But they weren't any longer, hadn't been for some time. They had grown up and took care of themselves. So even this had settled itself. But that morning Lothar Witte did not think of that either. Except for the moments when the memory of the extremely painful scene in Professor Tilius' waiting room yesterday afternoon kept coming back—and

Lothar had already developed a technique to forget it—this was actually a pleasantly unproblematic morning, disturbed if at all by the craving for a drink which kept nagging him. Since his mother was still delaying in the house, he finally took a sip of brandy from the flask he kept in the glove compartment. He felt the effect almost instantly; suddenly he liked the sight of the completely deserted street, shrouded in lightless, summery green, its pavement of small bluish-gray cobbles which neither reflected anything nor revealed a trace of a shadow, which was like nothing but itself, the dry, clean pavement of Frohnau near Berlin, silent under the roof of foliage screening the sky.

At last he saw his mother step out of the house and walk toward him, small and straight as a pole. Over her sharply crooked lower left arm she carried her raincoat, and her left hand clutched her worn leather purse and her gloves. How Prussian she looks, Lothar thought, as he leaned from his seat to hold the door open for her and watched her come down the garden path, with quick, precise steps, not forgetting to close the gate behind her with a brisk jerk. She seemed somewhat contrite at having, to her own surprise, kept her son waiting and, as always when she felt unsure of herself, put on an even more arrogant air than usual. But she isn't really arrogant, Lothar thought, it's only the impression she gives, because she has this tight little figure and a nose that looks as though she were descended from the Quitzows or Kottwitzes—when actually she only comes from a rectory in the Havel Marshes—and a mouth as concise as an ancestral motto. "She looks exactly the way you'd expect the widow of a Prussian brigadier general to look," Lothar's friends would say after they were introduced to her, at which point Lothar would reply crisply that on the contrary the brigadier general, his father, had not looked Prussian at all. "But like what?" someone might ask, at which point Lothar would sometimes produce a photograph showing the old gentleman at his headquarters during the Polish campaign shortly before he had been killed at the battle at Szamotuly in September 1940—a powerful, overflowing figure, so much like Lothar that the friend looked at the picture in embarrassment. For it was vaguely alarming to recognize an aged Lothar in the uniform of a senior infantry officer looking arrogantly at something that had obviously displeased him. Whether it was the war, a soldier's awkward posture or simply the weather, the elder Witte—whose only child Lothar, for reasons unexplained, had remained—gazed shortly before his death at something which life was holding out to him, just as Lothar might at times gaze at a friend, with cold, scornful interest.

"Where have you been all this time?" Lothar asked, as he helped his mother get settled.

"Oh, never mind," she replied, somewhat flustered.

He was not listening carefully and paid no heed when, after collecting herself, she added: "I had some trouble finding my gloves."

As they drove down the road toward Tegel, Lothar's mind went back to the brandy flask and he decided to take it out of the glove compartment and slip it into his pocket at the next opportunity. In the distance the flat roofs of the Siemensstadt factories stood out distinctly under a sky of almost white gray. A pleasant day, Lothar thought. He liked shadowless, neutral weather. The drive to Hamburg would be nice on such a day. His mother had been planning to visit relatives in Hamburg and he had offered to take her there; he was on vacation from the university and the little detour up north tempted him. The drive through the Mark and southern Mecklenburg would give him a

chance to revisit after many years parts of a countryside
that had once meant so much to him.

His mother had accepted the proposal, if with some
reluctance. "You know I don't much care for long drives,"
she had said, but Lothar knew she was afraid he might
start drinking on the way.

"Won't you tell me now how your meeting went yesterday?" she asked. "Are you going to get the job at Berlin?"

Lothar shook his head. For some time he had to keep
his mind on the traffic, then he said: "They don't want
me."

2

After completing this sentence, he saw himself sitting
once again in that Kurfürstendamm café where he waited
yesterday until it had been time to go and see Professor
Tilius. Despite the sunny day, he did not sit at one of the
outdoor tables. He sat inside, not in the dark recess of the
room, but by the large open windows where he was able
to watch life go by; not like a cave animal with bulging
eyes, lurking in the depths, but inconspicuously, in a
neutral zone of mingling light and shadow, in the realm
of half-light where he was able to think so well. He
watched the women at the sidewalk tables under the big
striped awning and followed with his eyes the ones passing
by on the boulevard; he wondered whether he should
strike up an acquaintance. But the brandy he was drinking
had already done its work: he sat heavily in his chair; a
few magazines which he had bought lay on the table before
him; he had meant to glance through them but could not
bring himself to do it; he kept thinking about his Göttingen lectures, with interruptions for an occasional glance
at some feminine apparition; fragments of dresses and hair
became mixed up with certain ideas of Amaury de Bêne,

who had died in 1206. The phrase *"omnia unum, quia quidquid est, est deus,"* suddenly came to mind against the background of a yellow confection from a Berlin couturier, around which a stylish black hairdo was blowing like wind; added to this were speculations on how much better it would be to live in Berlin instead of Göttingen. Lothar did not mind the provinciality of Göttingen, but simply the fact that Göttingen did not concern him, even if he occasionally did brighten it up with Lichtenberg. But then Lichtenberg himself would have preferred a professorship at Berlin to life at Göttingen. Lichtenberg was a dead man at Göttingen, while strangely enough Fontane was still alive in Berlin; and the fact that the roads to Neuruppin and into the Dosse Bruch were ignominiously closed did not diminish his presence. Sitting in his quiet café, Lothar paid homage to his favorite authors, reserved and austere, by placing them against their backdrop of wide avenues and landscapes of pine; at last he established a glance-relationship with a pretty dark blonde who sat facing him at a table outdoors, but dropped it after a few moments and fell back into his inertia. Once again he told himself gloomily that essentially there was something contradictory in his preference for austerity and fractured light; his great moments of half-light were invariably bought with alcohol, and even when the craving did not lead to intoxication it was a craving for something completely and utterly depraved.

He ordered another glass of Rémy-Martin—his third—and drank it slowly before rising from his chair. It was five, the sun was gone, and the time had come to go to the university.

In the hallway he ran into puffy, harassed little Tilius, beside whom Lothar seemed like a dignified country prelate, devoted to his studies and wine, come to lobby with a quick, glib *monsignore* from the cardinal's suite. To him-

self he called Tilius a philosophic windbag, a skillful ex-
ploiter and compiler of other people's ideas, author of
books with sensational titles, brilliant negotiator, strategist
amid organizational confusion, a man on the make—
Lothar's resentment for his teaching colleagues led him to
endless new definitions of the dean of philosophy, and his
talk with him proceeded exactly as he had foreseen: a
welcome of marked friendliness, pulled past the secretary's
desk into the dean's study—"Nice of you, my dear Witte,
to show your face here again!" Tilius' proficiently suave
talk and Lothar Witte's equally proficient question—pre-
sented in an ironic tone of voice and as though not meant
at all seriously—about a possible appointment to the Berlin
faculty, so strictly in line with academic rules and regulations that Tilius did not have to come out with a direct
refusal. Inserted into this procedure a quick exchange of
words in which things came to a head, in which—and they
both knew it—the die was cast after Tilius had asked:
"What will you lecture on next term?" "On some out-
growths of the movement of the spirituals in the late
thirteenth century," Lothar said. "Ramón Lull, Olivi and
others."

"Very interesting," Tilius said, but Lothar felt the
irritation in his voice. Tilius controlled himself. "A rather
offbeat subject," he said, "but no doubt certain parallels
to the present situation may have . . ." he broke off, seeing
that Lothar was already giving his reply with a majestic
shake of his head.

"On the contrary," he said with that ruling-monarch
irony his colleagues always resented so much, "what in-
trigues me is to point out situations with specific conditions that don't compare to anything else. In fact, the only
thing I am interested in is to explore how far a certain
development is unique."

This was the cue that offered Tilius a way out, and he

seized it and began to elaborate on the Berlin situation. Lothar hardly listened. As far as he was concerned the meeting was over; he had labeled himself a lone wolf, one of those eternal research professors whose philosophical studies occasionally cause a sensation but are too out of the way, on the whole, to justify a regular professorship. The critics called him either a "talented, often brilliant maverick" or, in more disparaging terms, "a remarkable mind frittering itself away." When Lothar sensed the note of guilt and hence impatience coming into Tilius' voice, he rose to take his leave. The only difference between this talk and others Lothar had had with Tilius in previous years consisted in the fact that today he felt a strong desire to stay in Berlin. When he had last applied two years ago, it had still seemed like asking for trouble, in view of Melanie, and the university's refusal had come as a relief, since he then still felt he would not be able to live in this city with his memories. That seemed to be over now and he deplored the fact that Berlin was closed to him. Perhaps I might apply as a research professor, he thought vaguely, as Tilius saw him out through the waiting room.

Having said goodbye, Lothar turned again in the doorway, half determined to say something to Tilius about a research professorship. He saw the secretary smile toward Tilius' room and make the gesture of drinking. Lothar stood aghast for a moment, staring at her; her face turned scarlet as she became aware of his presence and the gesture of her hand froze. Downstairs in the hall he had to sit down for a moment; he was white around the nose.

3

Lothar used the delay at the Staaken checkpoint to remove the brandy flask from the glove compartment. His mother went off to the shed of the border police while he lifted the suitcases from the car, and after he had seen her disappear into the building from the corner of his eye, he reached for the flask, took a quick swig and slipped it into his coat pocket. A policeman watched him do this, but indifferently; from his looks Lothar could not tell what he was thinking. With the man's eyes on him, he carried the suitcases into the shed. Methodically and silently the Vopos checked the luggage but found nothing in his mother's bags that caused them to ask questions; they took a little longer over the contents of Lothar's briefcase— books, notes—and exchanged muffled remarks among themselves before returning it to him, a certain wariness in their glances. At the exit an official told them about the speed limits en route and handed Lothar an instruction sheet showing the time by which he would have to report at the Ludwigslust checkpoint. Lothar put the suitcases back into the car. The day was still summery, overcast, light gray. When his mother had gotten in, he asked her to wait a moment and went off to the men's room. There he took another swig from the bottle before returning to the car. He rinsed his mouth with water, but after they had been driving for a while his mother said: "You've been drinking, Lothar."

"Just a small sip of brandy, Mama," he replied. "I felt a little queasy."

He knew she was now trying to decide whether to go so far as to ask him to hand her the flask, to keep it till the end of the trip; but he knew his mother well and figured she would humiliate her son to such an extent only in an extreme emergency, and he was right. However, perhaps his mother kept silent only because—they were just passing the barracks of Nauen—an army convoy came toward them, trucks with Russian soldiers. Despite the summer day, they wore long coats; they stood motionless, with broad steel helmets on their heads.

After they had passed, the road became very quiet, the intervals between passing cars longer and longer. Lothar felt that the liquor had come between himself and things—things inside and outside the car; reclining in his seat, as in a chair in a theater, he watched them from a certain distance; this gave him a false sense of security, but as he had had only a snifter, he still was able to realize that it was caused merely by the practically deserted road and the low speed limit. Still, it was pleasant to watch the passing irrigation canals, peat pyramids and lanes of birch from a sort of royal distance; Lothar even noticed the fine peat dust hanging over the countryside; how was it, now, that Fontane described it? For a while Lothar searched his mind, then he remembered: Fontane had called it the color of chewing tobacco.

"The Marshes," Lothar suddenly exclaimed, "Mama, just think, we're driving through the Marshes."

"Nonsense," his mother said, "we are driving toward Friesack. The Havel Marshes are to the south and the Wustrau Marshes are north, near Lake Ruppin." She really knows her way around here, Lothar thought. No wonder, after all it's where she grew up; what's the name of that hole again where her old man was a minister? Stechow.

"Shall we go to Stechow, Mama?" he asked. "It can't be more than twenty kilometers from here at most."

"For heaven's sake," she protested, alarm in her voice, "don't do anything foolish, Lothar! I've no desire to end this trip in a Russian Zone jail."

"But it would be so nice," he said, to tease her a little more, "to see if the rectory still stands and the old church."

"It wouldn't be nice at all," she retorted. "It would be

ghastly." Then, after a moment of silence, in order to close the subject, she said: "At my age one lives in one's memories. But one doesn't like to be reminded of reality."

She reached for her purse and Lothar heard a rustle of paper.

"Do me a favor," she said. "Eat something."

Lothar looked down at her hand, offering him half a sandwich. Her hand was frail, the skin freckled with brown age spots. He took the sandwich and bit into it.

"I know you hold your liquor well," she said, "but it is better to have something with it."

He knew she thought the opposite of what she was saying. He knew she thought that like all alcoholics he could no longer take even two or three sips without getting tight. Lothar felt the gritty, buttery taste on his tongue; the ham between the slices repelled him. Even with the first bite of the sandwich he felt that it was robbing him of some of the cold, clear mood given him by the brandy, and he laid it down on the seat beside him in disgust. From the corner of his eye he saw his mother give him a disappointed look, then turn away. She watched the countryside passing by at the prescribed speed. If she weren't so Prussian, he thought, she'd cry now.

"I don't know the Marshes nearly as well as you do," he said, to distract her and give her the feeling he was completely sober, "but I do know the Ruppin highlands." He paused and as he began to remember, reeled off names: "Rheinsberg, Lindow, Zernikow, Menz Forest, Molchowsee . . ."

His mother interrupted. She began reciting a nursery rhyme she had taught Lothar when he was very small. " 'Is it due north up Rheinsberg way, is it due south by Molchowsee?' "

" 'Is it Rottsiel in the vale?' " Lothar went on gaily,

while his mother watched him with pleasure. " 'Or Kun-
sterspring or Boltenmühl? Or Boltenmühl or Kunster-
spring? Has Pfefferteich the magic ring?' "

They both burst out laughing at the quaint awkward
names and at the fact that after so many years they remembered the rhyme supposedly long dead and forgotten.

Lothar was the first to fall silent, because the names
suddenly brought Melanie back to him with a jolt; indeed,
the names had a power that reality no longer possessed, as
the sight of the villa at Frohnau had proved this morning.
Its reality no longer roused any feeling in him, whereas
the mere mention of names like "Rheinsberg" or "Molchowsee" almost paralyzed him at the wheel, for a moment
nearly blinded him. For the names brought back poign-
antly certain walks with Melanie in the Havel country,
moments of exotic brown skin, silk of faded, clear colors,
snatches of conversation, coves with rushes, glances, creak-
ing pines, blowing hair, the reflection of a shadow. How
had his mother put it? "One doesn't like to be reminded
of reality." She had grown wise, his mother. She had no
desire to see her paternal rectory again. She did not want
to have her memories killed.

They found Friesack unchanged, arrested in motion
behind a few SED banners, frozen in a prewar pose in spite
of a Red Army war memorial with a Russian sentry standing guard beside it. But otherwise: the rectory, the school,
the mayor's office, the pub. Nothing glittering. The corner
store with a little blackamoor and a garland of sulphur-
string in the window. Otherwise nothing but dark red,
mud-yellow, gray, under the light gray sky. A small town
in the great Prusso-Slavic plain. Gone.

Lothar began to get fidgety as he always did when he
felt the effect of the drink wearing off. The pangs of flat
soberness wrenched him from the pleasant daze in which

the liquor had enveloped him. In his mother's presence he could not reach for the flask to wash down the hangover that was beginning. On the quiet stretch behind Friesack he tried desperately to retain the serenity the brandy had given him, but only the stabs of memory suddenly brought to him by the place-names could take his mind off the dreariness now possessing him. Glimpses of that time, which Lothar sometimes ironically called his "heroic years," swept past him like the peat bogs, rye fields, oak forests which were provoking them, and an irrepressible desire to find those years again, to recapture those years and Melanie—an irrational idea, half nourished by drink, half by soberness—made him for a moment remember on the road behind Friesack that a few kilometers further on, another road branched off to the north and led through the Rhin Marshes to Neuruppin.

He laid out a plan how to divert his mother's attention, and when he spotted the fork with the road signs he reached for the sandwich and started eating again. Shortly before the intersection he dropped it, as if by accident, and by the time his mother bent down to pick it up while he was busy with the wheel, he had passed the crucial spot and turned off the interzonal highway. When she handed the sandwich back to him after cleaning it in her meticulous way, he said, "Thank you!" and from then on watched her closely out of the corner of his eye. Since she rarely went anywhere by car, it did not strike her as unusual that the road had narrowed, and she also calmly accepted bits of cobblestone pavement, once even a stretch of open sand, remarking only once that the road was getting worse, though without seeming to suspect anything. They passed through several villages. But only when a sign at a village exit said "Neuruppin 15 kilometers" did she become alarmed.

Grabbing Lothar's arm, she said: "We are on the wrong road."

He did not answer immediately and she shook him. "You know the main road does not go by Neuruppin," she said. "You've taken a wrong turn."

By now Lothar no longer felt the effect of the drink. In such moments he always felt resentful, as though he had suffered a loss, resentful and reckless, and so he did not even try to conceal that he had deceived her.

"I'm doing quite all right," he snapped. "I'm just making a little detour."

"You turn around this minute, Lothar!" the old lady said. She was sitting bolt upright now. "You know we are registered. If we don't report at the checkpoint within the appointed time . . ."

She stopped out of a sense of dignity, the way adults do when they see that they cannot control a little boy's stubbornly bad behavior, with a shrug but at the same time hurt and sad.

"Just a very small detour," Lothar said. "We'll make the Ludwigslust checkpoint in plenty of time."

But his mother said nothing and he knew that after having had her moment of defiance she was now sitting very small and frightened beside him. I'm behaving disgracefully, Lothar thought, I'll turn around and go back; but instead he went on.

They passed through Neuruppin without being stopped. Two young policemen standing by the Fontane monument glanced lazily after the car. The wide squares of the little town lay empty in the pale noon. At the embankment Lothar took the road to Müritzsee leading over toward Mecklenburg, because his memory gradually began focusing on a piece of forest by a lake near a village called Klink, where he had once spent an afternoon with Melanie. He could just as well have gone to Rheinsberg or to half a dozen other places, for the whole area was alive with memories of outings with Melanie—sometimes alone with her, sometimes accompanied by her husband and children, whenever they had been able to talk Richard Brahm into joining them—but for some reason, perhaps purely by accident, Lothar's mind had in the last quarter hour fastened onto that afternoon at the lake near Klink, and so he drove the Opel further north.

When they were in the open countryside again, he looked into the rear mirror to make sure they were not being followed by a car. But the road was completely empty.

He heard his mother say something, but as he was wrapped up entirely in his own thoughts, the words barely registered.

"This is going to end badly," she said. Brittle and old, her voice broke the words like twigs.

4

Lothar had some trouble finding the spot he was looking for and in the end he recognized it only because he saw the lake gleaming on the right when he reached the forest behind Klink. He stopped to get his bearings. As in the days when he had come here with Melanie, it was a forest of tall beech trees with smooth trunks and light green leaves that still kept some of their springtime brightness; where the underbrush opened out on the edge of the forest the lake gleamed from the right. All the same, something seemed to have changed. Lothar finally attributed it to the different approach; with Melanie he had come up on foot from the village of Klink, carrying a beach bag, whereas today he had driven up in a car—that accounted for the shifted perspective. Besides, he remembered, the prewar day with Melanie had been sunny and windy, whereas today was calm and overcast; at that time the lake had been flashing with light, while today it barely gleamed, gray-blue under warm air which seemed to have thickened like milk in a bowl.

Lothar recognized the lane to the lake he had walked down with Melanie, and turning the car into it, followed it cautiously. He managed to park the car behind some underbrush by the edge of the forest, where it could not be seen from the road. During the entire operation his mother made no sound. When he switched off the engine, she calmly got out, spread her coat over a tree stump, placed her purse beside it, sat down and looked at the lake which was not very big, though big enough to convey a feeling of expanse. On the far shore one could see fields and woods, but no houses. "This is almost like Mecklenburg," Lothar said, "though we are still in the Mark." But his mother did not answer.

Lothar recalled that he had used exactly the same phrase to Melanie that time, but the recollection was just a mechanical click of his memory; it produced no vision of Melanie no matter how hard he tried to bring her to life against the present background. Finally he pulled out the flask and examined it. He had bought it yesterday in Berlin, a flat, slightly curved half-pint flask of French brandy, and it was still more than half full; in his mother's presence he did not simply put it to his mouth but poured the brandy into the aluminum cup, which also served as a screw-top, and drained it.

They heard the sounds of an approaching car in the distance and held their breaths. Lothar turned around and looked toward the road, but could see no sign of the passing vehicle; the underbrush obstructed his view.

"We are completely covered," he said when the noise faded away and was followed by new engine sounds. This time it seemed to be a truck, shuddering heavily as it went by. But after that everything became silent, they were alone again, and the quiet day lay motionless in the milky light above the water and the rushes.

The whole situation and the word "covered" roused vague and adventurous thoughts in Lothar. "We are partisans," he said, his face broadening into a half-grin. "I almost feel like a soldier. Funny, don't you think, that I should have gotten through the war so peacefully?"

His mother kept her stubborn silence and he went on thinking aloud without paying any attention to her; already the liquor was spreading inside him like a light weight, calming to his mind. "Never sailed through a war more splendidly," he said, mimicking the clipped jargon of the Prussian officers' clubs, "never joined the army, always held on to the job, always played it nice and cool." He knew how this line infuriated his mother but for a while he enjoyed showing this nasty side of himself, then suddenly dropped it. "For the first time in my life I am lying under cover somewhere," he said forlornly. His father had not insisted that he become a regular army officer, but had respected his son's intellectual interests. When his whole caste had come under a cloud, Lothar had blackmailed him; thanks to his old man's connections Lothar had been exempted from military service.

"I was a slacker," he said, "and I made Papa help me. Remember?"

Still she said nothing. Lothar knew how much he hurt her by bringing up these things. After all, the elder Witte's decline had been in no small part the work of his son; Lothar had made his father commit a corrupt act, unbecoming to an officer under any circumstances. In the eyes of the regime, the old man had been able to retain his mask of a Prussian brigadier general; but in the family circle it had disintegrated when Lothar, rather unscrupulously, appealed to his father's sensitive conscience by making his desire to evade the draft into a political issue. Perhaps it was this that had created that look on his father's face in the photograph taken before the battle at Szamotuly: a disgusted, arrogant look, a look of cold and disdainful interest, a broken look.

His mother finally roused herself to say something.

"Don't you think we might go on?" she asked. "Let's go back, Lothar, as fast as possible! If we are lucky and the police don't stop us, we may still get back on the road to Hamburg in time."

"It would have been better if Papa hadn't gotten me off," Lothar said. "If he had known what it was I had to do to keep out of the army!"

They had let him evade the draft and because he was a historian had assigned him for duty in the war archives. As a soldier I'd have only been their victim, Lothar thought, slightly boozed, staring into the rushes by the lake at Klink; as an archivist, I was their faithful servant. As usual he brushed away the memory of certain documents he had read then. He had read them, numb with horror, and then he had catalogued them. He had been neither a doer nor a victim, but had shunned the deed as well as the sacrifice; they had not let him off entirely but had forced him at least to catalogue the sum of the suffering. He had been a bookkeeper of inhumanity: the shoddiest role of all.

"Everything you did, you did because of Melanie," his mother said. "You were a slacker in order to be near her. You accepted being assigned to the war archives so as to remain in Berlin, with Melanie. She was your evil spirit."

He looked at her in surprise. Never before had his mother allowed herself to speak of Melanie in such a way. Not only had she never spoken of her like this before; she had, on the contrary, made it her tactic to take no position at all toward his relationship with Melanie Brahm. What prompted her to speak all of a sudden now, when everything was over?

"Yet, Melanie was not at all evil," she said. "I always liked her. Actually, she was a good woman." She paused, obviously groping for the right expression. "What I mean is," she finally said, "she was naturally kindhearted. You just handled her wrongly, you and Brahm. Perhaps she would have stayed with you if she hadn't realized that in the last instance all your decisions depended on her." Again the old woman paused before going on. "Perhaps she would not have run away from you after the war, if you had simply let yourself be drafted into the army. She felt that you took on a dishonest life in order not to be parted from her. Believe me, no woman can take that, Melanie least of all."

He could no longer bear the voice or the words it was speaking. He walked along the edge of the lake for a bit and lay down in a sheltered hollow on dry pebbled ground. There he really started drinking, slowly and steadily, in small sips which he let dissolve in his mouth.

5

There was not much motoring in those days before the war; at least not in the circles to which Brahm and Lothar Witte belonged. So Lothar and Melanie were walking from the Klink railroad station where they had arrived on the local train, having spent the night at Rheinsberg. Lothar carried—again he remembered very clearly—a linen

bag striped in dark and light brown which held her bathing suit and toilet articles, and as he let the brandy melt
on his tongue he wondered what could have become of
this memento; dusty, faded and dingy, it probably was
lying in the attic of the villa at Frohnau. Keeping completely still in his pebbled hollow, he waited, but to his
surprise the beach bag remained the only moving object
in all that faraway day of sun and wind, the only thing
alive; while the equally clear memory of Melanie having
worn a sports dress of stone-gray silk on this outing seemed
irrelevant, a mechanical observation, no more. His mother
was right: revisiting familiar places was not a good way to
invoke memories. The detour into the northern Mark
Brandenburg was as useless as it was dangerous.

So it was all over, Lothar recapitulated the fact he had
once before stated this morning while waiting for his
mother in the car: after fourteen years everything was over,
had to be over: Melanie's flight, and the years before, and
every single moment of those years.

He wondered whether he was too sober still to give his
mind the necessary turn that would unlatch the door
behind which Melanie stood and—perhaps waited for him;
he took another swig from the flask, but it was no good
and he knew as he was drinking that to fill himself up
would not help at all: because there just wasn't any door,
there wasn't even a wall separating him from Melanie.
There was just a big empty space around him, a space
conspicuously marked by Melanie's total absence.

As often in such cases Lothar tried to help himself by
registering dates: in 1938 it had been a twenty-three-year-
old Melanie who had walked with him to the lake at
Klink—he had met her in February '38 at a costume party
in some villa at Grunewald—she had then been in her
third year of marriage with Richard Brahm and had had

her first child the year before: little Andreas, who was twenty-four now, had completed a few courses of sociology, economics and history at the university, and, undecided, indifferent and highly talented, had finally settled for a job in some European agency at Brussels. The dates began to arrange themselves in groups above the straw-yellow of the rectangular fields and the squares of forest-green on the shore across the lake. When the war had come, a year after that 1938 summer of joint expeditions, Lothar's son Günther was born, a boy who strangely enough was interested in practical problems, studied typography and at twenty-two worked as a sales specialist in the printing business. In 1943, right in the middle of the war, there was another child still, Richard's daughter Marianne. She was eighteen now, looked like her mother and would finish school next year. This sounded, Lothar thought, as though everything had gone smoothly with the children, but actually things had been tough for Richard and myself, the children had been as difficult as children can be—are there ever any children who are not?—but ours really were particularly difficult; come to think of it, they still are, but they are grown up now and take care of themselves. The children had been a headache. Lothar took another drink and then he thought that this lake reminded him more of Mecklenburg than of the Mark Brandenburg before he went on to think that it must have been a wonderful feeling for Melanie to walk out on three children and two husbands. She was thirty-two when she disappeared without a trace in October '47. The children had then been ten, eight and four. She left us in the lurch, all right, Lothar thought, and she is forty-six now; how does a woman feel at forty-six when she remembers that somewhere she's got three children, three children she doesn't know anything about? While he drank Lothar realized that he hated Melanie.

"Come on, let's go swimming," Melanie said to him, and he was not even surprised that now she was with him after all. She sat by his side in her white bathing suit, hugging her knees and peering out over the water.

"I'd rather wait a while," he heard himself say. Dressed only in his bathing trunks, he looked down at his large body, which even then had a tendency to overflow. Lothar was not fat but there was something ungainly about his powerful body; he had never been able to wear ready-made clothes. In the gray, hot, overcast light he gazed at his skin—not pale but almost colorless—a skin of uncertain color on a big, indolent body which had to make an effort to remember that it had muscles, which liked to withdraw, to be immobile. His heavy bulk wanted to wait a moment longer before plunging into the water, but when he looked at Melanie, he found that the light had changed. Now it no longer was the neutral half-light from the high, even ceiling which had made it hot and humid all day; it was the deep east-wind gleam of that day twenty-three years ago, made up of broken bits of ultramarine sky, chrome-yellow wheat, and the Indonesian batik-brown of Melanie's arms, legs and shoulders, with her bathing suit left white in the center—a gouache like an early Pechstein. Melanie's hair, tied up in a pony tail, was hanging down her back. She was all watchfulness, tense, straining for the element; and so there was nothing for Lothar to do but get up. She skipped ahead of him across the narrow beach of round pebbles, then with a cry flung herself into the wind-whipped dark waters and began to swim on her back, quietly, silken like a fish. Once in the water, even Lothar's body became supple, the body of an elegantly slow, heavy sea mammal. He swam far out into the lake and from out there watched the shore, the beech forest and the reflections of the tenuous white clouds.

Melanie's head suddenly emerged by his side. She had swum some distance under water and was now shaking the drops from her sleek dark brown hair. Silently they circled each other for a while, until Melanie said: "It must be deep here." At this her eyes suddenly filled with unreasonable fear and she swam back to the shore, where her fear dissolved and they continued drifting about for a long time.

Later, lying on the beach while their bodies dried in the sun, Melanie did not say what she said sometimes in later years: "Too bad Richard didn't come." Her acquaintance with Lothar had been too young for such a remark that first summer; their arrangement *à trois* had been an established fact from the very first moment, but Melanie certainly had no regrets that Richard Brahm cared nothing for scenery and hiking but preferred now and then to sit out a night in a bar with her, quietly discussing his affairs, the affairs of an able but reckless man of business who loved finding new productive forces to exploit. Melanie had a feeling for both things: the Black Bottom bar and the lake at Klink, Richard's business and Lothar's introverted and tense attitude toward historical studies. The two men, having ascertained their sympathies for each other, had come to a tacit understanding; even their political convictions were a link and both felt instinctively that there was something in their agreement about Melanie that defied the current trend toward power, force, possession, toward oppression, and the general tendency away from freedom. But the times were getting darker despite the fact that there were days like this: love-days on east-wind shores.

"One day I'm going to leave you, you and Richard," Melanie said. "Believe me, I'm going to leave you."

Again Lothar reached for the flask. The air was no

longer a pleasant half-light, just a dirty pale gray, a whitish gray, disgustingly without color. His mother still sat on her tree stump, stern, distressed; he could see her through the underbrush, sitting there motionless. Then, once again that other day appeared, the picture in opaque colors.

"Why?" he asked. "What's the idea? You have absolutely no reason."

They were lying side by side, Lothar on his back and Melanie on her stomach; with her head on her folded arms she was brooding in the crook of her elbow. Raising her head, she looked out across the trees and said: "There will be a war. And after the war, times will be very different. When those other times come, I'm going to leave you."

He felt the round pebbles under his back. Even in those days he had been drinking, though in moderation. He did not remember what he had answered Melanie. Incidentally, she had often made such remarks; he really had no reason to blame her for anything—she had been honest right from the start. Nor had he any reason to hate her. But he did hate her. By now he was so drunk that he knew once again why he hated her: because he never had been able to make out why she left him and Richard Brahm and the children that October in 1947.

During the years when they were still talking about Melanie, Richard and Lothar had made this a subject of almost scientific discussion. First of all, they deliberated, of course, whether the cause of Melanie's decision had been another man, but they had not found a single trace pointing in that direction. Was it Lothar's dipsomania, Richard's reckless business operations, that had finally undone her? Melanie was a woman who accepted or rejected a man for what he was, and she had accepted both Richard and Lothar, had lived with them and had understood the merits of their shortcomings: the wild extrava-

gance of character showing itself in both Lothar's bent for
the bottle and Richard Brahm's risky speculations. Was it
really just a kind of violent, naïve curiosity for life, together with a stubborn conviction that a new age called
for a new life, that had prompted her to make that jump?
Lothar could not believe it, nor had his disbelief been
shaken by the fact that she had remained totally irretriev-
able despite all the efforts the two men had made to trace
her.

Did that mean that his mother was right? "Perhaps she
would have stayed with you if she hadn't realized that in
the last instance all your decisions depended on her." "All
your decisions"—in his mother's way of thinking this
meant, of course, Lothar's decision to force his father to do
something disreputable; which meant to her the con-
temptuous melancholia which had driven Brigadier General Witte to his soldier's death. "She felt that you took
on a dishonest life in order not to be parted from her."
Yes, they had certainly done that: lived a dishonest life,
Lothar as a bookkeeper of death and Richard, too, who
after all made money from the war. But had Melanie left
them because they had taken on something for her sake,
or for a much deeper reason which his mother was unable
to understand: because Lothar and Richard did not fit
into Melanie's blind concept of an entirely new age,
because the new life waiting here for her in the depths
of the dark age could not be shared with two men who
had dirtied their hands with the old? Does she now live
in the new age, in the clean age, Lothar wondered? I am
still living the same old way. "For the first time in my life
I am lying under cover somewhere," he had said earlier.
But that wasn't true. Actually he had spent his entire life
under cover. He looked around. In Prussia you were
always lying under cover. It was to be hoped that wherever

she was living now Melanie had found that new life where she could move freely, holding her head high.

He wanted to get up and challenge his mother, ask her again what had prompted her to call Melanie an "evil spirit" and a "good woman" all in one breath, but the weight of the liquor held him. Melanie had disappeared and he had only one more glimpse of her standing by the edge of the water. Again she was wearing her dress of stone-gray, faded silk. Barefoot, she stood with her back to him, wringing out her white bathing suit. Her sleek, wet hair glistened; she must have been in the water a second time.

A ripple of slenderness and South Sea brown—Tahiti-brown astray on North German summer lakes—of stone-gray silk and yearning for a new age ran over her supple body like water. Sitting drunkenly at the edge of the forest, Lothar felt how this gesture once and for all crushed his most profound aim in life, his desire to live in pleasant half-light, to linger motionless in the quiet light, to observe and to think. Lasting but a second and consisting of nothing more than brown skin and gleaming water, the gesture had been more powerful than the most strongly developed side of his character. The picture dissolved— Melanie had not turned to him again—and Lothar looked at the flask which still held a bit of brandy. This, too, had power over him, had destroyed his liking for a life in a discreet, inconspicuous atmosphere, his determination to stick to neutral zones.

Finally he managed to get up. He screwed the top on the flask and put it in his pocket. Noticing how drunk he was, he went down to the edge of the water, wet his hands, scooped up some water and splashed it over his face. He dried himself with his handkerchief. Then he went back

to his mother, trying hard not to stagger on the way. She
looked up at him.

"What actually did you mean," he asked, "just now,
when you said those things about Melanie?"

He managed to say the sentence coherently, but he did
not know that his voice was the raw, deep voice of drunk-
enness and carried a drunken threat.

His mother was not afraid. She stood up.

"Give me the bottle, Lothar," she said. "You have had
enough."

For a moment he looked as though he was going to hit
her. Of course, he would never have hit her, not even
when dead drunk, but it was a savage scene, depraved and
ugly in the bright, hot, sunless light.

"I am quite all right," Lothar said furiously. "I am no
longer a child. I am no longer your child."

6

She paid no attention at all to what he said.

"I had a letter a few days ago," she said, "a letter from
Melanie. That was why I kept you waiting this morning,
Lothar, not because I was looking for my gloves. I was
wondering whether I should take the letter along and give
it to you."

Suddenly Lothar saw nothing but his mother. She wore
an inconspicuous gray suit, proper widow's clothes; but to
him she seemed as though cut out of bright cardboard and
pasted onto a foil of white paper. Around his mother the
world was empty and white.

"And?" he asked eagerly. "Did you bring it along?"

He saw that she nodded. After staring at her a moment
he said: "Give it to me!"

"You give me the bottle," she said, "and promise that we shall go back this minute! Then I'll give you the letter."

Reeling forward he lunged for the purse, still in its place beside the stump among rocks and grass. As he bent down he felt a dead weight revolving in his head.

Then something strange happened: his mother began to fight for the purse. As he held the old, brown leather thing in his hands, she clung to it and tugged at it without a word. She gave him a desperate look as she did this and in her eyes was something tugging also, a look of wild, helpless humiliation. Lothar had never before seen his mother lose control; he was so taken aback that for a moment he became almost sober. Overcome, he let go of the purse.

They stood facing each other, Lothar with his mouth open, his mother breathing heavily from her effort. Suddenly there was a stir in the underbrush by the edge of the water. At once their eyes became wary, and Lothar spun around while his mother stared past him at a spot in the bushes where something seemed to move.

Then a man emerged. He was short and stocky and they both took an instant dislike to him, although he turned out to be friendly. In the Low German of Mecklenburg he said: "I saw something when I came down the road. Thought to myself, that's a car down there."

He was dressed in a blue suit, as if he was going to a fair or a funeral, and had a seaman's cap on his head. With an expert eye he examined the car, especially the license plate.

"You're from the West," he stated.

"Yes," Lothar said, "we are on our way to visit relatives."

The man nodded. He had a smooth, fat, solid face. In spite of the heat he did not seem to perspire in his blue suit. His eyebrows were tow-colored, his eyes a cold china-blue, and his lips pouted a trifle. Lothar knew the man would be able to smack his lips.

"Where are you headed for?" he asked so casually that Lothar felt the smack behind it.

The question took Lothar by surprise; he needed a few fatal seconds too long to collect himself; at last he produced the first name that came to his head: Prenzlau.

The man nodded, obviously satisfied to have his victims in his grip.

"Prenzlau," he said, weighing the name in his mind.

"But then you've gone all wrong if you came by the Berlin road. You are much too far west. Why didn't you go via Oranienburg?"

"We wanted to make a little detour," Lothar replied.

Now they would find out whether or not the man was an enemy. Lothar was prepared to see him pull out a police badge any moment.

"Detours are dangerous," the man said. And after a pause he added: "In our part of the country!"

Still the tension persisted. The man prolonged it by going down to the water, picking up a flat pebble and watching it skip several times across the surface before sinking. He was evidently a pebble-skipping champion. That's a lousy bastard, Lothar thought, drunk as he was, a lousy bastard of a stool pigeon. He remained standing and tried to keep steady so as not to show the man the condition he was in. His mother stood motionless in the crisp, arrogant attitude that had become second nature to her.

The man came back.

"If you'd rather go back to the West," he began, then continuing quickly and pointedly with a calm observation that obviated all discussion, "because you have lost your way," and completing his sentence with a suggestion: "then there is a good road from here."

Lothar breathed a sigh of relief. Even his mother stirred slightly, indicating that she was beginning to relax. So the man was not an enemy; on the contrary, he was a helper. Not a very friendly helper, for he remained cold. He seemed to register with a sort of cold, smacking relish that the shock caused by his presence was diminishing—but never mind.

He moved close to Lothar. "Drive on a bit further," he said, "but not as far as Barrentin." He spoke without lowering his voice, but he made it toneless. "Just before Barrentin a road turns off left, down to the lake. There is a ferry across the lake. From the other side it's only a few kilometers and you'll be back on the interzonal highway."

"No Vopos?" Lothar asked. He now no longer restrained himself.

The man's hard, china-blue eyes glared with hatred. But he controlled himself, just shrugged and said, "If you're out of luck!" He was a helper. The strange thing is, Lothar thought with alcoholic clairvoyance, that I don't like him any better since I know it. However, a disagreeable helper is better than an agreeable enemy, he thought; you can't choose your friends.

"And the ferryman?" he asked. "What's he like?"

"The ferryman is all right," the man said.

There was no reason to ask further questions, but Lothar still remained where he was, embarrassed to let the man see what was wrong with him, for his first step would reveal that he was barely able to stand up.

"Thank you," he finally said. "Thank you for the advice."

The man turned without a word, walked back to the edge of the water and began skipping stones again. Lothar literally stumbled toward the door of the car, pulled it open and collapsed on the driver's seat. The car had been standing in the heat and Lothar broke into perspiration. He rolled down the windows before starting the engine.

His mother followed slowly and seated herself beside him.

The man had stopped skipping stones; he stood and watched Lothar from a few steps away.

"Is there anything I can do for you?" Lothar asked him. "Anything you need? How about money? West money?" The offer came awkwardly, with drunken rudeness; all Lothar's dislike of the man was in it.

"Lothar!" his mother said.

The man just looked at him coldly, china-blue and fat. The seaman's cap sat straight on his thick tomcat head. He says the ferryman is all right, Lothar thought, but he himself is not all right. Something about the man was far from all right. In his drunken stupor Lothar suddenly, before he got the car started, began to be afraid of the man. The car rumbled slowly out into the lane. In the rear mirror Lothar could no longer see the man.

As he stopped the car briefly before turning onto the road, his mother said: "I'd much rather you took the road we came by, Lothar!"

"But why?" Lothar asked. "His tip is first-rate, if it's correct."

Only then did it strike him that his mother had not said a word during the entire incident with the stranger. In all that time she had seemed as though in a state of shock.

"I have a bad feeling," the old lady said.

Lothar shrugged his shoulders. "We won't get through Neuruppin a second time without being stopped by the Vopos."

While his mother was saying, "Now I'd almost prefer having a run-in with the police . . ." he turned right, in the direction the man had indicated. He stepped up the speed of the car. Being drunk, he drove with excessive accuracy, keeping the car sharp on the right; his eyes were fixed on the road through the forest—which to Lothar consisted only of diffuse, green light through the beech trees cut by a meticulously drawn gray road. They met no car. Once they passed a woman pulling a cart piled with twigs.

Not until much later did he remember about the letter again. The thought of Melanie's letter came back to him with such an impact that his attention was diverted from the wheel and the car careened over to the left of the road. He straightened it out, then asked: "Why didn't you give me the letter back in Berlin?"

"It is addressed to me," his mother replied, "and meant for me. I don't even know whether Melanie would approve of my letting you read it."

"Ridiculous!" His voice became harsh. "One of Melanie's tricks. Obviously she wants to make contact with Richard and me. She's just trying to make it more interesting."

He felt that he was mad with desire for the letter. It was unbearable to have this letter within reach in his mother's purse right in the car. Only a last remnant of self-respect kept him from stopping the Opel and asking his mother to give him the letter. In revenge for having to control himself, he began accusing his mother.

"She's acting just the way she did in those days," he sneered, "when she would have these long, friendly talks with you before she came to see me, at Frohnau, you remember? She knew I was going crazy while she was chatting with you, that I was aching for the moment when she would come to my room, but she dragged it out, she made conversation with you. She never said so, but I think she looked down on me a little because here I was a grown-up man, still living with my mother." And to fill the cup to the brim, he added: "Perhaps that is another reason why she left me: because I did not part from you until long after the end of the war."

"Yes," his mother said, and if he had not been drunk, he would have been struck by the completely detached matter-of-factness in her voice. "Perhaps you should have separated from me in time and should have taken Melanie away to live with you. Away from Richard, too."

But Lothar did not listen. Suddenly he realized that he had passed a road sign saying "Barrentin, 2 kilometers" and that just before that an unmarked road had turned off to the left. He stopped the car with a jolt. "But not as far as Barrentin," the man had said. Lothar looked back; the signpost was still visible. Gently he began to back the car up. In his stage of intoxication the maneuver was almost too much for him; zigzagging all over the place, he backed the car to the entrance of the road. Once, with the Opel almost at right angles, he sat for a few seconds panting at the wheel: he felt dead drunk and started sullenly brooding.

Half a pint of brandy, he thought, that's nothing really, but I'm as tight as a tick, like any alcoholic who instead of getting immune to liquor gets more defenseless all the time. Two or three sips can now do me in, he thought, staring disconsolately into the depth of the forest before he pulled himself together. His mother watched him in silence.

The road to the lake where the ferry was supposed to be was narrow and unpaved, a small white forest road. It was afternoon, the light had changed, the sky above the tree-tops still shimmered, evenly white, but the rays coming through were fractured; a pleasant gray had spread which made it almost look like rain. So Melanie is back, Lothar thought, just by letter for the time being, but she is back; I shall read the letter as soon as we get onto the interzonal highway; feeling relaxed now and in control, he set himself a course of action: the ferry, then the few kilometers through the Dosse Bruch—wonderful advice the man at Lake Klink had given him—then the road to Hamburg. Once back on the road he would stop the Opel for a moment and read Melanie's letter. It was only natural that all this should bring back Melanie's farewell. She had called him one morning in October '47 right after breakfast and asked him to come over. Richard was away on business and Andreas and Günther were at school. Only little four-year-old Marianne was in the apartment with Melanie. Melanie asked him to keep an eye on Marianne that morning; the cleaning woman would come at noon and by evening Richard would be back, she said, but she had no one to be with the child in the morning and she had to go on a trip.

Lothar had been annoyed. "Why?" he asked. "Where are you going?" "I have to go on a trip," Melanie had said, "just on a trip. I don't know if I'll come back." Already in her cloth coat, she stood outside in the hall brushing her hair. Her suitcases were packed and ready to go and she left the apartment without another look at the little girl who was playing in the living room. Like everybody else, Richard Brahm and his family had lived in rather cramped quarters in 1947. Lothar had gone into the living room and looked down into the street where Melanie got into a waiting cab. The cab went off, leaving the quiet residential street completely empty. Lothar had turned away and settled down in an armchair in the living room; for a long time he had watched little Marianne playing quietly with her building blocks, paying him no attention. It was the time when toys for children were scarce.

7

The road led into a large lumber yard on the edge of the lake. Peeled beech trunks were scattered about and the ground, covered with chips of bark, made a crackling sound when Lothar drove down almost to the edge of the water. He saw the cable strung across the lake, which might have been about 1,500 yards wide at this point. The ferry was on the other side, a sort of raft, as Lothar could see after he got out. There were no houses on this lake either, at least Lothar could see none from where he stood; only the chimney of a brickyard showed above the woods, quite far to the north.

Lothar formed a cup with his hands and called: "Hey! Ferryman!" But nothing moved. He called again. Finally he went back to the car—his mother had not left her seat—and sounded the horn. It made an ugly noise, hoarse, tortured. On the other side a man came into view, emerged from the forest and leisurely pushed the raft off the bank with a pole. The ferry was connected with the cable by two ropes and Lothar noticed that the ferryman pulled the raft along the cable, using no oars. In the gray afternoon light the lake was so quiet that the ferry seemed not to move. Lothar looked at the rushes lining the bank where he stood; a thin froth lay motionless between them, no breath of air stirred the chips of bark floating on the lifeless water. Lothar waited, a glazed look on his face; he would have liked to finish what was left in the flask, but drink had made him limp and he could not rouse himself even to make that effort.

It took the man ten minutes to cross the lake. As he approached he turned out to be a tall, gaunt figure dressed in the gray linen customary among the Wends. He addressed no word of greeting to Lothar. The raft was made of tree trunks covered with boards, and after it had run ashore, the ferryman put out two planks so that the car could get onto the deck. He stayed on the raft and watched Lothar manipulate the car.

"A primitive contraption," Lothar said to his mother, as

he started the engine. "It's only here in the East that they still have things like this." Yet deep inside he was delighted by the simple raft, the Wendic ferryman, the mysterious, secluded lake.

"Wouldn't you rather get out?" he asked.

She shook her head. Lothar glanced at her and again felt uneasy when he saw how withdrawn she looked. He realized that she considered the car a kind of protection; everything about this trip had been frightening to her and she now wanted to stay in this tin shell until it was all over, until she was safe again. I have behaved like a bastard, he thought.

The gray raftsman had put the boards neatly to fit the Opel's wheels and Lothar managed to get the car onto the deck at the first try. Relieved at this proof of his skill, he got out of the car. The man pulled in the planks and started the ferry moving. To his surprise Lothar noticed that there was already a rapidly growing expanse of water between himself and the shore. The ropes from the ferry were running silently on wheels along the cable. The man had nothing to do except pull at the cable, and this did not seem to require much strength even though the raft now carried the weight of the car. He stood with his back to the deck while he was pulling and looked out on the lake, but without seeming to see it.

Lothar moved up to him and began to help pull. The rope felt hard and smooth. For the first time the man opened his mouth.

"Stop!" he snarled. "You don't know how to do it. People who haven't learned to pull just get the barge into trouble."

Startled, Lothar let go. In fact, after he had touched the rope, he had felt a tremor go through the craft. Now he tried to decide how the ferryman's voice had sounded. It had sounded like the voice of a very old man. The man was tall and gaunt and looked like an old man, but not like a very old man.

The lake could be seen now in its full length. Toward the south it ended in a wasteland of rushes, in marshes commanded by a few solitary pines; toward the north was a cove of beech forest. In the far distance farm roofs showed red through the foliage: those must be the houses of Barrentin. There was no church steeple; the chimney of the brickyard had also disappeared. The afternoon lake gleamed in the Brandenburg summer light: silent, dreamlike, silvery. Only the wheels were making some small noise.

"We are from the West," Lothar said. The man's silence annoyed him and he wanted to find out if he could break it. Like all drunks he wanted to talk.

He got no answer. News of this sort did not seem to interest the gray man. As a matter of fact, Lothar had expected this. He tried a direct question.

"How long have you been running this ferry?"

The raftsman did not look at him. Stubbornly he went on with his work. But he deigned to reply:

"More than fifty years."

Lothar tried to work it out in his mind and arrived at the figure 1910. The Empire, the Republic, the terror, communism. The systems. He must be almost seventy. That's why his voice sounds so very old, Lothar thought. Gone through four systems with a ferry in the Mark Brandenburg.

"Were you in the army?"

"Yes, in the first war," the man replied, "not in the second." He came out with something more, a thing that seemed important to him. "It was a good thing somebody was here in the second war. When the people began to flee . . ." He broke off, fell silent.

As usual when he was tight, Lothar had inspirations.

One should write history, he thought, based on the testimony of this kind of a man. People should tap a completely different set of sources besides reports from ambassadors, letters, memoirs. How do four systems of government, four different ideas on how to rule, appear on a remote raft deep in the heart of the Mark Brandenburg around the middle of the twentieth century? Material for a Ph.D. thesis! If I had students working on their Ph.D. I would chase them out of the archives into the open air to interview someone like this. Once again he realized somewhat bitterly that nobody had asked him to judge Ph.D. theses. He was a research scholar dealing with remote subjects, a specialist on certain aspects of medieval history, set on the idea of demonstrating the uniqueness of a historic process, a quiet scholar, a quiet alcoholic, a lover of half-light, and obviously a failure as a man, or else Melanie would . . .

He was about to finish this thought in order to remind himself that Melanie might be coming back. Then he intended to turn to the car window and tell his mother about the seventy-year-old ferryman who had worked here since 1910—this kind of a life story would have gratified her pride in Prussia—when again a tremor passed through the ferry; first he felt it in his feet, which suddenly became unsteady. He was standing at one end of the ferry, still looking back to the shore they had left. It was far away by now. They must be crossing the middle of the lake, and because the tremor he felt in his feet did not stop at once, he took a step backward and turned around.

It is possible that Lothar Witte realized at the very moment he turned around that the car with his mother inside it was rolling toward the forward end of the ferry. It is possible but it is not likely. It is just possible that the retinas of his eyes revealed the Opel, which had in fact started rolling, as it rolled along slowly and almost gently, yet within a fraction of time hard to determine because of the very short distance it had to cover, so fast was this slow roll, until it reached the edge of the ferry where it tipped into the water front-wheels first, then plunged forward top-heavily and disappeared with a sudden gurgle. But the picture on Lothar's retina does not seem to have carried a message to his brain immediately—being too remote, probably, from anything Lothar then regarded as reality. It did not fit into the life he had lived, a life which, in spite of drink and in spite of his passion for a woman, probably had been a rather quiet one. This may explain why Lothar, after the plunge of the car and the great lurch of the ferry made him fall to his knees, remained there, his hands grasping the wet boards, remained on all fours, staring at the spot where the Opel had been. It was gone, but it could not possibly be gone.

The gray ferryman had a similar reaction. He had noticed that something was wrong because the ferry suddenly resisted his pull; but he was too slow to turn around immediately, and then the great lurch had made him cling to the rope. Clutching the rope, he did not fall as Lothar did. His eyes just caught a glimpse of the car disappearing in the water. He let go of the rope and silently looked across the empty deck. On the cable above, the wheels crunched back and forth.

When the old man saw Lothar get up and take a few steps toward the edge of the deck, he went and grabbed him by the arm.

"It's no use," he said. "The lake is three hundred feet deep here."

Actually, Lothar had had no intention of jumping into the water in an attempt to rescue his mother. He simply wanted to look at the spot where the car had sunk, although he told himself at once that perhaps this no longer was the spot at all, that the ferry had probably moved far past it. He ran to the other end and looked down; the water was an even dark green all around. It was too early still for him to imagine his mother's body lying down there, but nothing could have moved him to touch this water with any part of his body.

"Can the woman swim?" he heard the ferryman ask him. "If she can swim she might still come up."

Lothar slowly turned his head in the speaker's direction. So this old man actually suggested that he should picture his mother down there trying to squeeze through the car window to get up to the surface, perhaps making a last desperate effort against suffocating, against the water filling her lungs. He sat down on the planks of the ferry and doubled up.

"No, it's impossible," the man said, suddenly realizing what he had suggested, in his Low German and his very old voice. "That far down she must be dead by now." And after pausing a moment he asked: "Was that your mother?"

Then he pulled the ferry along. It was lighter now and a few minutes later they tied up on the other side. Lothar remained on the raft.

"I'll go and phone the rescue people," the man said.

Lothar looked up. "Tell me, why didn't you notice I was drunk?" he asked crossly. He now spoke to the ferryman as though to an inferior. "Why didn't you notice I had not pulled the hand brake or put the car in gear when I had it on the raft?"

"I don't know about cars," the man said drily.

He said something more, but Lothar no longer listened. He looked across the water. Only after a time, long after the man had disappeared, Lothar's brain finally formed the message which had stayed so long as a picture on the surface of his eyes. It was not the picture of the rolling car, not its plunge into the deep water, not the white bubbly gurgle it had stirred up in the dark green. It was the face of his mother which had stared at him for a split second before the Opel, disappearing headlong, snatched it away. His mother must have turned around in her seat when she felt the car rolling. There had been no time to cry out. She had simply turned around, very surprised probably, perhaps not even frightened. She had looked at Lothar as if to ask him for an explanation, more amazed than horrified. And so she had disappeared, an unspoken request to her son on her lips. Lothar clearly recalled the expression on her face. On the edge of Lake Barrentin, squatting on the planks of the ferry, it began to become part of his past, and he welcomed his mother's last face into his memory by starting to laugh.

At dusk the rescue squads arrived from Wittstock. They brought their diving gear and there was also an ambulance. Lothar, still laughing, was given an injection by a doctor. When they lifted him into the car, he was already asleep.

He got over his shock rather quickly. They took him to a jail in Berlin, and because they did not really know what it was all about they treated him as a political prisoner awaiting trial. The cell where he was in solitary confinement was lit night and day, so that he had little sleep. At ten-thirty at night he was given two blankets and allowed to lie down. He was not permitted to cover his face and hands and whenever he did so unconsciously in his sleep, they woke him.

He tried several times to explain why he had strayed from the interzonal highway, but they looked at him uncomprehendingly. During one inquiry the examining judge told him that the car had been raised and was being confiscated by the police.

"What about my mother?" Lothar asked.

"She has been buried," the judge replied, "in the Witt-stock cemetery."

"We have a family plot," Lothar said, "in the Herrenhut cemetery at Blücher Platz."

"You can always arrange for a reburial later," the judge suggested.

A few days later they brought him the items that had been found inside the car, mainly things that had belonged to his mother, among them a brown leather purse. These showed that they had been in the water for a long time and had been dried conscientiously. They seemed like exhibits, archaeological finds, mummified.

Inside the purse he found Melanie's letter; the envelope had been stamped by the censor. Lothar looked at the letter; he read his mother's address written in Melanie's hand. Her handwriting seemed to have changed very little. The ink had run here and there from the wet. Without reading it he tore it carefully into tiny bits.

Three weeks later he was discharged. Tilius had cleverly intervened on his behalf via colleagues at Humboldt University. They took him in a car to Brandenburger Tor where he was met by Tilius, who had been notified. At this meeting Tilius showed himself at his best, not at all deanish, no suave talk, rather silent and obviously affected by Lothar's misfortune. When they were sitting in the taxi he said: "The East Berlin prosecutor is going to send the documents to the West. You'll probably have to face a suit for causing death by negligence. But you'll almost certainly get off on probation," he added. Lothar asked to be dropped at Bahnhof Zoo. Before he got out, Tilius said: "Couldn't you quit drinking, Witte?" He spoke like one man to another, the way it should be.

At the station Lothar asked for the schedule of the

interzonal trains. He made up his mind to return to the West the next morning. Then he went to see a broker and arranged for the villa at Frohnau to be sold. The house had no mortgage and the broker indicated that he would get a good sum for it; Lothar figured that with the money he could take a few years' leave of absence from the university to write his book on Amaury de Bêne. He walked down Kurfürstendamm and ended up at the Bristol Hotel. The Bristol terrace was heated by infra-red rays. Lothar sat on one of the cushioned wicker chairs and, shaded by the awning, looked out on Kurfürstendamm. Women were carrying umbrellas of different colors along the rainy boulevard. After the weeks in jail where he had been given nothing to drink Lothar impatiently waited for the brandy he had ordered. He drank carefully and not more than two glasses. Then he went off to find a hotel room for the night.